Almost Forever

Lilian Stead

Copyright © 2025 by Lilian Stead

All rights reserved.

No portion of this book may be reproduced in any form without written permission from the publisher or author, except as permitted by U.S. copyright law.

Contents

Chapter 1

S ophie

The plane touches down right on time as I look out the small window at the night lit up by the overpowering lights of the airport. We taxy down the runway and I close the small window that is the porthole to my old life, sliding the barrier physically between the two worlds and wishing I could do it as easily emotionally. I take the last sip of my small inflight cocktail and close my eyes as it burns my throat and warms my insides. It will be the first of many burns I know I'll be feeling this week.

The other passengers begin to spill into the isle and I can hear the sound of the compartments above my head opening. I'm not getting out of my seat until I have to. Let the frantic old ladies and tired whining children out first. I'm not going to fight for a position in that miserable line when I can sit in this uncomfortable seat and prolong the last few moments I have to myself.

The man that was sitting beside me stands up and I open my eyes to make sure his departure does not include his carryon being dropped on my head. With a small smile and a nod, he steps into the aisle amongst the crowd and makes his way to the front of the plane. I have to admit that I've been a terrible seatmate. I was not really a big conversationalist and his attempts to start friendly chitchat fell flat as I kept a steady flow of alcohol streaming over my lips and wetting my tongue.

Finally when the last person has left the plane, I stand up a little wobbly and reach for my carryon. I can tell the flight attendant is anxious for me to get off this damn plane so she can too. I straighten out my skirt and feel the ache of standing in my heels again. I hadn't had time to get out of my work clothes before rushing to make this flight. With my bag in hand, I exit the plane and take the long walk up the jet way feeling my dread build as I take each step.

It isn't horribly late for a Monday night, but the airport is still pretty empty and there are small areas where the shops have closed and the lights are shut off. Of course there is no one waiting for me, I didn't really confirm with Rachel what time I'd be arriving for that exact reason. I think it's for the best that I get to the hotel and check in alone so I can have a night to let the events of this next week really settle in my head and heart.

The baggage claim area is a little more crowded, but only a few bags are still making the rotation. I watch my black bag with the pink ribbon I had attached to make spotting it easier, make a turn and move in my direction. When it gets close, I grip the handle and pull it to the floor beside me. This is it. I have arrived and a few hours from now I'll be facing my childhood best friend and the rest of her bridal party at the hotel restaurant for brunch.

The air hits me like a tepid wet breath, sucking the air from my lungs and plastering my face with a moist sheen of perspiration. Yes, I'm back in Florida for the first time since leaving four years ago. I have about six days before I'll be stepping back off of an airplane and into the fresh California air. I just hope I can survive this week with my sanity and dignity. Right now it doesn't feel like either are possible.

I pull the wedding invitation from my purse and hail a taxy at the curb. The driver pulls over and helps to put my bag and carryon into the trunk before returning to his seat. The smell of fake leather and old air freshener offends my nose, but I know I must smell like a bar towel so I try my best to pretend it isn't hard to breathe, and switch straight to mouth breathing only.

"I'm going to the Marriot." I move to show him the invitation, but he waves it off and pulls into traffic so abruptly that I slam back against the seat. Fine, I guess he knows exactly where it is. I make it about two blocks before I have to roll my window down despite the horrid wave of uncomfortably thick air I know is going to come sweeping in. I hate humidity. I'm sure my sleek, long, straight California hair is quickly becoming my frizzy, fluffy, Florida hair.

When I finally step into the lobby of the hotel I let my head fall back and enjoy the crisp air conditioning for a second before righting it again. I tip my rolling bag into a slanted position and pull it behind me to the counter. I reserved my room under the wedding block a few months ago and now I'm having second thoughts about being so easily attached to all the other people in the wedding party. Being inconspicuous sounds the safest, but I know the right thing to do is go along with Rachel's plans since she has been planning this big day since she was twelve.

I try to travel the hallway on my floor as quietly as possible. My goal is to be alone and not folded into the arms of some acquaintance I was happy to leave behind when I boarded that plane four years ago and headed to California. Once in my room, I quickly kick off my heels and slip on a pair of flip-flops. I pull my hair over my shoulder and braid the strands so I can maintain some semblance of control over it.

My short-sleeved, blush pink, silk blouse has seen better days, but where I'm going it doesn't matter. I open the minibar and pull three small bottles of vodka from their shelf and tuck them into my bra. I have a date with the moonlight and I'm not going down there unarmed. In ten minutes time I'm sneaking back out of the room and making my way to the pool.

The large sign on the gate warns me the pool closed ten minutes ago, but I still push the gate open and find a chase lounger at the edge of the crystal clear blue water. The lights above are shut off in an attempt to deter rule-breaking guests like myself, but really they have no chance of stopping me. I sit down and adjust the back of the lounger so that I'm sitting up enough to drink my liquor and also reclined enough to relax and see the stars.

The sky in Florida doesn't look much different than the one I can see from my balcony in California. I find that very comforting tonight as I listen to the insects chirping in the grass on the outskirts of the pool gate. The first bottle goes down a little rough, but that's probably because it is more like my eighth or ninth of the day. The next one goes down much smoother and my shoulders relaxed as the thoughts that have been circling in my head bleed together and get fuzzy.

I close my eyes and listened to the sounds of the night as the alcohol makes my muscles warm and pliant. The creak of the gate opening gets my attention and I slowly lift my eyelids to see who has broken the calm of my private sanctuary. A small light is shining in the distance and the peace is further broken when a man bites back a curse, but lets loose a growl as his toes make contact with the hard metal frame of a lounge chair.

"No, no, I'm ok," he says into the phone that is shining on the side of his face. "I just kicked something. Fuck that hurts!" He doesn't see me as he limps in my direction and I try hard not to find his half limp, half hop attempt at moving hilarious. Alcohol can blur the lines between mildly amusing and completely gut-busting. When my snickering breaks the night air between us, his face quickly turns in my direction and he comes to a complete stop.

"Let me call you back," he tells the caller. He moves the phone from his ear and taps the screen.

I'm trying to pull it together, but I can't stop laughing. "I'm sorry," I manage to say before another bout of giggling bubbles out of me. I wipe at my eyes, sucking in a few breaths to try to put an end to the cackling.

"You're not even trying to contain yourself," he teases, and I'm pretty sure I snort from the ridiculousness of this whole situation.

"I'm sorry." I reach into my bra and pull out the last small bottle. I look down at his feet in the darkness and wonder why he hadn't at least worn flip-flops. He starts to approach me slowly and I watch as this man in an expensive suit tries to walk like his recently smashed toes aren't hurting. He almost pulls it off, but a few feet from my chair he starts to hobble again and then lets an impressive chain of expletives fly as he spins around and plants his ass in the chair next to mine.

I tip my head back against the vinyl straps of the chase and lift my small bottle of vodka in his direction. "This might help." His lips curl into a smile and he takes the bottle from my hand. When his skin touches mine the tiny hairs on my arm lift and I can feel the sensation all the way up to the back of my neck. He twists the little blue top off the bottle and sighs.

"It won't be nearly enough, but it's something." Before he drinks it he reaches up and loosens the silk tie around his neck then leans and adjust his lounger to match mine. Finally he tips the small bottle back and swallows its entire contents in one gulp.

I watch him stare up at the sky for a minute before I turn my head back to the moonlight and try to not notice the way he smells like soap and the fresh woodsy scent that is always uniquely male. I think I also smell power and money--but it might just be the alcohol. I would never claim to be an expert in men. This week is going to really drive that message home.

He tucks the small bottle into the pocket of his perfectly pressed shirt and then reaches for his wrist. He struggles for a minute with the button and I realize that he's almost as tipsy as I am. I hold my hand out for him to put his wrist in and he only hesitates a brief moment before allowing me to help with the button. When it's freed, he moves his other wrist into my grip. I pop the button through and try to ignore how nervous and excited it makes me to touch him. His closeness floods my senses with rich cues that seem to speak to my female brain and nerve endings without permission. I manage to release his wrist before I turn to goo.

Pulling the sleeve down to gain a small bit of tension, he expertly rolls up his sleeves and then unbuttons the top two buttons on his collar. "Thank you." His voice rolls over me and I love the way it burns as warm inside me as the alcohol had.

"It's the least I could do for laughing at your expense," I tease.

He nods. It's quiet for a moment as we sit beneath the night sky. Under any other circumstance this would be an excellent way to meet someone. It has just the perfect amount of amusement and attraction. The problem is, there's already a history between us. Not a love story, just a few years where this man, Andrew, had a friendship with the man I was in love with. We were together quite often during that time.

"Do they know you're here? I wasn't sure you were going to come." He slowly turns his head to look at me, but I keep my eyes trained on the sky above. Just like that the weightlessness and ease of the evening suddenly becomes heavy and insufferable.

"No, and I wasn't sure I was going to come either." My answer doesn't require any more explanation than that. He already knows why I don't really want to be here. My heart aches in my chest as the reality of what I'm going to have to take part in this next week sinks in a little deeper.

"If it's any comfort to you, I think Rachel and Evan have worse boundaries than Facebook." While he says it in a serious tone, I immediately laugh. I don't know that a truer observation has ever been said. When I turn my face towards him he's looking right at me. He smiles, but I see the empathy for me in his eyes. "You should have told them to fuck off."

"Perhaps," I say with a sigh. "But then I wouldn't have been the bigger person. Who knows? Maybe this is something I need to see." I shrug a little and watch his face become clearer as my eyes continue to adjust to the darkness around us.

"Sure, but did you have to watch it from the front row? Shit Sophie, you're the maid of honor." He shakes his head and breaks our eye contact to look back up into the sky.

Rachel and I have been best friends since kindergarten. For years we had been inseparable. I always knew I would be the maid of honor at her wedding, just like I imagine she should be mine. However, what I never could have imagined is that she would be marrying the man I was in love with. Maybe one day I'll say it's for the best, but as of today, I'm not quite there yet.

Chapter 2

Andrew

I still can't believe she came. If I were her I would have told Rachel and Evan to go hell. I might never know the truth about what happened between them that finally ended their two-year relationship, but I know my best friend made the worst mistake of his life when he let Sophie Richards walk out of it. I'm not sure if he ever stopped thinking about her, but I know I haven't. If she wasn't my friend's ex, I would have tracked her down and fought hard for a chance to have her myself.

Evan and I have been friends since grade school. I don't always agree with his choices, but when he started bringing Sophie around our junior year of high school, I was jealous he'd found her first. She's so beautiful. Her hair was a bit shorter back then, but still the same dark brown shade that it is now and her eyes are crystal blue and hard to look away from. They would have kept my attention much more if her body hadn't also been something that made every male head around turn and stare.

She didn't go to the same school as us, so I was only able to see her when Evan and I would throw a party or double date. Sophie has seen me date a parade of women, but she has no idea that she had set the bar so high for other women, it was hard to keep someone that wasn't as great as her around long. I told myself years ago I would find someone that would make my heart race and my thoughts scatter like she did—and to this day I'm still looking.

I blow out a breath laced with vodka thanks to her small attempt at making my toes feel better. It didn't help at all, but how do you say no to something she pulled straight from her bra. Shit, I was so flustered I couldn't have even come up with a nice way to decline it. I was trying hard not to ask if I could see that move again. So now, I'm sitting outside in the humid night air in one of my best suits just because there's pretty much nothing that could pull me away from the sweet scent of her perfume and the slight hint of alcohol I can smell on her.

"So, you and Evan are still friends. That's good." Her voice is quiet and raspy and damn if it doesn't make every part of me light up with desire. My eyes are getting more adjusted to the darkness and I can see the way the small lights of the hotel rooms shine down to reflect off of the smooth skin if her exposed legs. What once were miles of teenage perfection are now the smooth and sleek curves of a woman. I let my eyes trail up to the hem of her skirt before remembering I should probably say something in response. If only the blood would reroute itself back to my brain.

"Yea, still friends. We don't spend as much time together as we used to, but we've traded football for golf, and try to find time to get a few holes in once a month." My phone rings again in my pocket and I know it's Evan wanting to finish our phone call and hear the last details of the bachelor party. I don't give a shit. "What about you? Still as close to Rachel?"

Her laugh is music to my ears, but then I hear the hurt in her chest as she sighs. "Sure. As close as we can be living different lives on separate coasts." She pulls her feet up a little and I wonder if she remembers she's wearing a skirt. A quick glance around at the empty courtyard lets me relax.

"I'll never understand women." How could they still be friends if Rachel dated her boyfriend right after they broke up? I expect her to argue with me or tell me it just makes them far superior to men, but instead she closes her eyes and shrugs, pulling the pale pink fabric of her shirt higher and exposing a tiny sliver of skin at the waist of her skirt.

"I don't understand them either. If I could, I'd resign from my sex effective yesterday. I guess there are those of us that break the rules and ask for forgiveness and lucky for them there are some of us that value the friendship enough to fall for it." Her honesty makes my heart clench. She's trusting me and maybe it's just because she's drunk, but I'll take it.

"Resigning from sex sounds pretty serious," I joke, earning me a light slap to my chest. She knows I know exactly what she meant. "But seriously, Sophie, how are you going to watch Evan marry her?" Her eyes meet mine and I see the evidence of hours drinking in the whites of them. Maybe she wasn't having as easy of a time being here as she first appeared to be.

"With the help of my friends." I can feel my brows pull together in question and the most brilliant smile shines at me from her moonlit face. Her hand lifts between us and she tosses me the small empty vodka bottle. Catching it, I chuckle and then nod. "But I'm afraid my room is all out of vodka and I might need to borrow some of yours."

My mind shouldn't go there, but of course it does instantly. I can imagine us in my room, the soft curves of her body beneath my palms and my mouth on hers. I know she'd taste like alcohol and the sweet flavor of six years of longing. I've wanted her since the first day I saw her and the four years that have past have done nothing to extinguish the heat that races though my body when I look at her.

"I do believe I saw three of your little friends hanging out in my wet bar," I tell her.

She laughs, and this time it's light and bubbly like before. Very breathy and dramatic she exhales, "I've been looking all over for them." I know it's very late and I want to stay out here with her all night, but I believe the girls have some event in the morning while the boys will be headed to the golf course. I hope if I ever get married I remember how fucking ridiculous it is to hold your friends captive for a week to celebrate a ten-minute ceremony.

I sit up and feel the piercing throb of pain as my hurt toes hit the concrete. I can't help the sharp intake of breath through my teeth. Sophie sits up at the sound and worries her bottom lip between her teeth before speaking. "We should ask the front desk for a first aid kit. It's probably best if you tape those two together incase they're broken."

I stand up and extend my hand to her. She doesn't hesitate to put her palm in mine and allow me to pull her to her feet. There isn't a lot of room between our chairs, which gives me the perfect excuse to have our bodies so close together. I can feel all of her pressed to my chest and I let her hand go so I can let mine trail down her back and rest just above her ass. I watch her register my touch and feel her chest expand with a deep inhale.

There's no way I'm going to let on how much pain my stupid foot is in as I guide her through the hotel lobby and up to the front desk. My bare feet pad across the tile. I had kicked off my shoes and socks before leaving Marty's room and our friends gathered there to party, to go down to make a few calls away from everyone. Finding Sophie alone by the pool made my injury worth it.

The woman behind the counter listens as Sophie explains my toe situation and I watch her, taking in her every movement like I've been starved of them over the years. When a roll of white medical tape is slid into her hands, she thanks the worker and we turn towards the elevators. "What floor are you on?" she asks reaching for the bright button on the wall.

"Third. You?"

Her lips form into a sly smile. "Third." The doors open and we step inside. I lean up against the wall to take some of my weight off of my quickly bruising toes. She moves right beside me and rests against the small handrail that circles the entire elevator. When the doors open again on our floor, I pull the room key from my pocket and watch intently as she slips hers from her bra.

We step into the hall and I point to my room a few doors away. "Come raid my mini bar. I have an early tee time and won't be needing any more tonight." I slide my key into the knob. She follows me into the small room and I make my way over to counter near the mini bar. Opening it, I tip my chin to her in invitation to choose what she wants.

Her perfect fingertips walk across the tops of the small bottles and I love the way she plays innocent when she chooses the three mini vodkas and tucks them into her bra. "Thanks Andrew. The next round is on me."

"I'm going to hold you to that." There are actually a lot of things I want to hold her to, or more accurately against.

"Sit down on the bed and I'll tape your toes." She moves towards the bed and I follow, grateful to lift my aching toes from the ground. She kneels down in front of me and I take the opportunity to really study how she's changed since the last time I saw her. I didn't think it would be possible she could've ever grown more beautiful, but she has.

Her fingers lightly wrap the tape around my injured toes and then she stands up and tosses the tape on the dresser. "There. Now maybe they won't move around so much." She brushes her long bangs from her face and rests her fists on her hips. "I better get going. I've got to be down at brunch by nine." I move to stand and walk her to the door, but her hand splays out across my chest and stops me. "Don't get up. I'll let myself out. If you need anything I'm just across the hall."

She holds her room key up and smiles. Most of the wedding party is on this floor, but knowing she's just across the hall from me will make staying in my room difficult. "Thanks. Good luck tomorrow." I pull my tie a little looser and lift it over my head. Her hazy eyes follow my movement and I can't help the small smirk I have on my face. When my fingers reach for the tiny buttons on my collar, she shakes her head slightly as if to shake off a thought, and then quickly turns around.

"Night Andrew."

"Good night Sophie," I reply knowing my night would be so much better if she stayed.

Chapter 3

Sophie

After peeking through Andrew's peephole to make sure the hallway is clear, I quickly dash across the hall and into my room. I set the small bottles on the table with the hotel stationary and room service menu. My head is a bit fuzzy still, but I can't quite figure out where the buzz from the alcohol stops and the intoxication of being so close to Andrew starts. This is completely unexpected.

I've been around Andrew before, years ago when I was dating Evan, but never had his voice settled so low in my gut and his touch cause goose bumps to climb up my limbs. Maybe it's just the alcohol, but there was definitely something different about the way his eyes were looking at me. I felt like he was suddenly everywhere, his presence a welcomed warmth on my skin.

My mind flashes back to all the innocent encounters I had with him over the years. We had been at the same parties, shared many of the same friends and yet this is the first time I felt like he truly connected with me as someone other than my boyfriend's best friend. I like it. Maybe I shouldn't, but tonight it felt good to have him here with me. Lots of people in the wedding party know my history with the groom, but Andrew seems to understand how hard coming here was even if I'm trying to pretend like it isn't the hardest thing I've ever had to endure.

Closing my eyes and blowing out a deep breath, I lie back on the bed and let the sleep I had been putting off finally take me. I know I'm destined to have nightmares about my time with Evan like I had for a full year after we broke up. I'm pleasantly surprised when there are no nightmares and instead dreams of Andrew fill my mind. I let his hands touch me and feel the heat from his skin on mine until I think I can't take the increasing tension building between us. Instead of reaching that moment I so desperately need where he finally puts his strong lips to mine, I awake to the sound of my cell alarm ringing from beside me on the bed.

With a groan and a hard pounding inside my skull, I open one scratchy eye to see it's time to get ready for the brunch I need to be at in an hour. A hot shower does little to make me relax as the thought of seeing Rachel and all of the women that know our history makes my stomach flip and roll. I lather my skin in my favorite vanilla and gardenia lotion I brought to remind myself that California is only a few days away. Of course that takes no time at all compared to how long it takes to blow dry my hair.

When I finally have my make-up on, I take a step back and long look in the mirror. I tell myself I can do this. I decide my lack of sleep and the red in the whites of my eyes makes me appear a little harsh, so I opt to curl my hair in an attempt to soften my look. By the time I slip my short lavender dress on I'm almost late. I tug the hem down after pulling on my wedges and grab my purse.

I hesitate for just a second before hitting the bright button to call the elevator. I still have time to back out of this. I know it would make me a royal bitch to ditch my friend and abandon my duties as her bride's maid, but maybe I never needed to really come back here anyway. The sound of the elevator doors opening startles me and my eyes race up to see who it's delivering to my floor. If it's someone from the wedding then my last chance to slip away from this whole thing is gone.

His eyes meet mine and his face softens as he steps out of the elevator. He smiles slightly, but then I guess the panic on my face has him second-guessing his initial reaction. "Good morning, Sophie." Andrew stands in front of me as I try to stop the spinning of thoughts through my mind.

Before I can stop myself I blurt out softly, "I'm trying to decide if I want to do this." His eyes stay trained on mine and he nods his head slowly as the doors to the elevator close behind him and it leaves to pick up another rider. I realize what I've shared and laugh without humor, pressing my palm to my forehead and looking away from him. His hand reaches out and takes my wrist, pulling my hand back down to my side.

"I'll never tell anyone you were here." He is so close to me now I can smell his cologne and the scent of the soap he used this morning. It's all mixing together into a delicious fragrance that seems to be slipping past my panic and planting itself firmly in my mind. He releases my wrist and leans in a little close to me, "You don't have to do this."

"I know," I say, but it sounds as defeated as I feel. "I don't know what I want anymore. I thought this would be what I needed to let the whole thing go, but now I just want to run again. What if I can't do this? What if I want to leave but I'm trapped at a table with those women? I might lose it in front of all of them."

He smiles at me again and I feel his soft laugh rush over me like a wave of heat. "Not the Sophie I know." His head shakes slowly side-to-side. "The Sophie I know wouldn't let catty women run her out of anywhere. I don't know what happened to that confidence, but it used to be in there."

I can't help but smile at his words. He's right. I used to be so confident. When Evan left me, he took that piece of me with him and I hadn't been able to get it back yet. Maybe that's why I hadn't dated anyone else since him. "I haven't been that girl in a really long time," I admit, my shoulders slumping a little at the realization.

"Give me your phone." I don't question him. I unlocked my cell and hand it over as the lights above the elevator began to climb in our direction. He calls his cell and lifts it up so I can see. "You have my number now. Whatever you decide we're in it together. You bail and I deny ever seeing you. You stay, and I will be here if you need me—anytime and for anything." I nod my head as the doors open and a couple steps off, forcing Andrew and I to move aside into the small corner of the hallway.

I'd like to say I don't notice the way his hand touches my hip, guiding me as we step away from the opening doors, or the way he uses his body to shield my identity from the mysterious couple until their unfamiliar language tells us they are not apart of the wedding. I let out the breath I'd been holding and I look up into his piercing green eyes.

I know I need to do this because I can't live another minute of my life afraid of starting something new with someone. I need to let all of the hurt from my past go so I can have a shot at happiness with someone else. "I need to do this." I expect some sort of judgment in his eyes, but what I find there instead is admiration. He's looking at me like I'm doing something far more amazing than just attending the wedding of an ex-boyfriend.

His hand on my hip pulls me a little closer to him until I feel his hard chest against mine. His cheek brushes my cheek and his lips hover just inches from my ear. I close my eyes and take it all in, the way my heart races and my breath speeds up, the dizzy feeling in my head and of course the heat where his hand is resting on my hip. "You're far more beautiful than she is. You face those women with the grace that you've always carried and know not one of them has ever come close to holding a candle to you."

My knees feel weak and I know I tremble when his hand presses against my hip enough to put some space between us. I take a minute to gather my thoughts before I look up to his face again. When I finally do, every ounce of doubt I have been feeling about being able to survive this brunch flees and the only thing I can think about is how I have never noticed the small scar on his chin and the way his hair falls so imperfectly perfect against his forehead.

When the doors begin to close again he steps away from me and holds them open. "It's up to you Sophie," he says with a small shrug. I push my shoulders back and step into the empty elevator. I stand facing him after pressing the lobby button. He moves his hand into his pocket and smiles at me, standing right in my line of sight until the doors finally closed between us. The drop of the elevator is nothing compared to the drop of my stomach as I replay his encouraging words in my head. By the time I step into the lobby, I'm sure my face is flushed from his compliment and the blood that's pounding through my system with the fluttering beat of my heart in my chest.

I see Rachel before she sees me as I enter the large restaurant in the lobby. She's wearing a pale yellow dress and I watch as she laughs with the woman beside her. When I move to the space on her other side, the voices at the table seem to extinguish like the flame of a blown out candle. She stands quickly and wraps her arms tightly around me. For a minute I hold her back, missing the way this used to feel so natural instead of forced and awkward.

I think the thing that stings the most is having almost lost them both. Clearly Evan was no longer mine, but if I hadn't been OK, or pretended to be OK with them dating, our friendship would've been over too because dating Evan was more important to her than all of the years we had invested in our friendship. For the first time in a long time it hits me how true that is. My heart clenches with the pain that our friendship means more to me than it ever meant to her.

"You look so pretty," I tell her when we finally pull apart. She smiles at me and turns us to the large table full of watching women.

"You all remember Sophie!" Her voice is cheerful as she wraps an arm over my shoulder and pulls me against her. "Here, I saved you the seat beside me." That feels nice. Knowing she had faith in me to show up enough to save the seat beside her gives me a little relief. I sit down and smile at the women who quickly turn back to their conversations. Rachel leans in and whispers, "I've missed you, Sophie." I want so badly to believe it's true so I turn to her and pulled her into another hug.

The brunch seems to pass easier than I had thought it would, but I find myself disinterested in the conversations around me. I feel the vibration of my phone in my purse and discretely check the incoming text.

Andrew: How's it going?

Sophie: OK I guess.

Andrew: Good. I was just checking because I found some more of your friends in my room. Guess they know the maid.

Sophie: Things are looking up. Now if this brunch could just wrap up. I want to hit the beach before the bar tonight.

Andrew: Need me to save you?

I don't get to answer him before my phone is ringing in my hands. Now that it isn't in my purse, the melody rings out as it vibrates against my palm. I see Andrew's name on the screen and can't help the smile that crosses my face. A few of the women give me disapproving looks, but I just answer the call and put it to my ear with an innocent, "Hello, this is Sophie Richards." I never answer my phone like that unless it's a work call, but no one at the table knows that.

"Sophie Richards, nice touch," he tells me. "Say 'Well I'm at a very important event.'" I fight the smile I feel tugging on my lips again. Instead I try on a serious face.

"Well I'm at a very important event." I look in Rachel's direction and notice her attention is right on me. I mouth, "Sorry."

"Good, now say 'Hang on, I'll need to check my book.'"

I glance around again trying to decide if I am really going to do this. Who am I kidding? "Hang on, I'll need to check my book." My heart begins to race and I meet Rachel's eyes again. She gives me an understanding look and motions for me not to worry. A few of the conversations at the table begin once more and I notice my phone call is falling into the background amongst the various voices fighting for their moment at this estrogen heavy table.

Andrew's voice slips into my ear again and I wonder if he can hear the way my breath has sped up with his entrancing voice and the lies we're now in on together. I glance into the lobby and catch a glimpse of him as he stands near the front desk. This time I know my lips curve up and I look away before I totally blow this chance to get away. "Now," he says calmly, "say 'Damn, I left it in my room.'"

"Damn, I left it in my room," I repeat. Rachel looks to me again and I shrug a shoulder. She motions for me to go ahead, whispering that we were almost through anyway. I nod my head and stand.

"See, I gotcha." He sounds so confident I can't help but laugh as I leave the restaurant and head in his direction. "One more thing," I can see his face from across the lobby but I'm not close enough to hear him yet. I tip my head to the side and raise my brows. His smile is as smooth as butter as he lifts a vodka bottle, "Your friends invited me to the beach. Hope that's cool." I smile so much bigger now and pull the phone from my ear as I pass him and step into the open elevator.

As if we don't know each other, he steps in beside me and we both look straight forward as the doors close. When we feel the small hiccup as the elevator begins its ride up we're finally free to laugh. I feel the relief of getting the whole moment with Rachel and the women over wash off of me as his rich laughter seems to move over my skin and sink in some place deeper. When the doors open, I step out and turn to face him in the small hallway.

"Meet me at the beach entrance with my friends in twenty minutes." I turn towards my room and walk the few steps to my destination. I slide my key into the door, telling myself not to turn around even though I feel the heat of his stare on my back. He watches me until the door of my room shuts with a click. I have no idea what I'm doing, but it sure feels better than watching my best friend glow with the excitement of marrying the man I thought I would spend forever with.

Chapter 4

A ndrew

I sit on the small wall that lines the walkway to the beach waiting for Sophie. After golfing with the guys this morning I was trying to talk myself out of knocking on her door. It wasn't that I had a grand plan about what I would do when she answered; I just had this tension in my gut that wouldn't let me go into my room without seeing her again. Finding her when I stepped off the elevator had taken any indecision out of my hands.

When she'd left me this morning to go to the brunch, my plan was to hang out in my room and maybe make a few calls for work since being here was forcing me to juggle my usually busy work schedule. Going down to the lobby to ask about receiving a fax changed my day in a very good way. I watched from the lobby as Sophie sat in the restaurant with Rachel and the other women. She was pretending to be happy, but there were a few small tells that showed she wasn't as comfortable as she was pretending to be.

I wasn't sure she was going to go along with my plan to rescue her, but it was worth a shot if it meant I got to hear her voice again. Now that she was probably on her way down to meet me like she'd arranged I feel a little nervous and excited. If Evan knew where I was and whom I was meeting he would be livid. I think his plan for this week is just to be nice to her so that Rachel didn't continue to work so hard to smooth things over with the friend she totally backstabbed. His plans for Sophie did not include me hanging out with her.

The hotel doors slide open and I see her thin figure as she steps out into the sunlight. Her long, tan legs seem to go on for miles under that silky blue cover-up. My eyes float up to the tie above her hips, currently cinching the fabric and showing off her perfectly tapered waist. I feel myself shaking my head a bit, wondering how Evan ever though Rachel was a better pick. The cover-up dips low on her breasts and I follow the thin straps of her string bikini up her chest to where it disappears to tie behind her neck.

She is every man's wet dream. Stunning and seductive without even knowing how she affects the men around her. I notice a few of the male staff in the front of the hotel turn slightly in their positions to watch her as she steps off the small curb and begins her walk in my direction. I stand from my position on the wall and give a small wave so she can see me. Her smile lets me know when she has.

She makes me feel like a teenager again. I find myself looking away from her and trying to focus on something else. It's something I used to have to do every time she was around. She was my best friend's girl, which means she was off limits to even look at too long. What a shame. All those years I had wasted the beautiful vision that was often right in front of me out of respect for a guy that ultimately screwed her in the end.

"Do you mind if we walk away from the hotel a bit? I got a text letting me know that a few of the women were going to come layout in front here and I don't feel much like jumping back into that group." Her words are coming out in a rush and I feel my heart pump with the knowledge that being around me makes her a little nervous. I think I like that, knowing that I'm having a similar effect on her as she has always had on me.

"Lead the way. I'm free until the bar thing tonight." I can tell my expression shows my distain for this whole week of kidnapping. Her small chuckle brings my eyes to hers again.

"I'm free until then too. Am I picking up on a little disapproval of the wedding events schedule?" She pulls her bag up a little on her arm and we begin walking down the strand away from the hotel.

"I don't understand why couples have to extend this out so long. I had to try to shuffle a bunch of my regular clients

around to make sure I could attend all these little 'moments'."
She's smiling and nodding along with my words.

"What ever happened to a small bridal shower and then a night out with the girls before the big day? Why must we follow the bride around like some entourage as she eats each meal and gets her nails done? For fucks sake, I have a normal life to live while she floats along in this fairytale of a week." Hearing the cuss slip out of her perfect mouth makes me laugh. She's summed it up perfectly and I couldn't agree more.

"It kind of takes the shine off the big day. I think by the time we are all standing there with them in front of all the guest we are going to want to strangle each other. No group of independent adults should be forced into nonstop group activities with people we probably don't hang out with on a regular basis for a reason. Having a mutual friend doesn't make us besties." This time she laughed out loud, earning us a few looks from the other beachgoers on the strand.

"Do you think Rachel would buy the excuse that I have a hang nail or some type of contagious nail fungus? She scheduled a group manicure right in the middle of the day tomorrow and it's really ruining my plans of getting a tan before I stand next to her magnificent dress in the horrible monstrosity she chose for those of us who will be standing beside her for the entire day and a party to most of the pictures that will be taken."

I reach out and slip my hand around her waist quickly, pulling her against my side just in time for a kid to come flying by on a bike, narrowly missing her. Reluctantly I let her go and she nods and smiles at me. It takes me a minute to remember the conversation now that I have felt her so close. My brain is lit up with a million thoughts of what she might feel like under the silk of her cover-up. I clear my throat and look out at the beach to get my thoughts together. "I think you have a shot with the fungus. I'd totally but it. And I'm sure you will look great in whatever she picked out." I don't chance a look back because I know how my compliments so far have seemed to embarrass her.

"Well, I'm not so sure about that. The dress looks like an upside down cupcake with all these layers of horrible ruffles." She grabs her sunglasses out of her bag and slides them on. "She totally did it on purpose. If I wasn't so sure about the design alone, the color sealed the deal. Burnt orange." She says it like I have an idea of what that might be. Not even a small idea but I know that I have never seen her look ugly so it would really have to be something awful to make her fears even remotely valid.

We are now a good distance from the hotel and I know that the girls Rachel hangs with wouldn't walk down here so far away from the safety of the rooms just incase they needed to touch something up. I see a small group of teenage boys check out Sophie as we walk by, but she is so stuck on trying to describe the color that she doesn't notice. "Well, it's a horrible color. It's so terrible that it actually has the word 'burnt' in the description." When her hand falls to her side after tucking a strand of hair behind her ear, I tell myself to man up and grab it with my own.

It's probably the only time that holding her hand could be played of as something minor. I tug her hand in the direction of the opening to the beach. It's just a few steps, and I release it as soon as our feet touch the hot sand. I try to hide my smile when her eyes look into mine, and I keep my pace towards the water so she doesn't have time to over think it.

I unfold the towel from under my arm and lay it in the sand at my feet. Her towel is spread out right beside mine. I pull my shirt off over my head and roll it in a ball to use as my pillow. I can see from the corner of my eye that she's watching me and it makes every flex of my muscles feel a little more forbidden. It also gives me an open invitation to watch her slip out of that cover-up.

Her long fingers reach for the tie and I watch as she pulls it away from her. I also look around a second so I don't seem like her every movement is drawing me in, but in reality it is. The tie starts to flutter in the small breeze as she reaches for the hem that drops just below her ass and rides along her tan thighs as she moves. She slips it up to her hips, allowing the dark blue bottoms to peak out from under the material before she quickly readjust her arms and shimmies the silk up over her perfect breasts. This time I don't' look away. No one can blame me; it just isn't possible.

She tucks the cover-up into her bag and pulls out a bottle of sunscreen. I immediately send up a prayer of thanks to whatever god is making this moment happen. She sits on the towel and begins to smooth the lotion over her skin. I sit down beside her and watch as she enticingly rubs her hands over every inch of skin that she can reach. Then of course comes the good part. With a shy look, she hands me the bottle. "Would you mind getting my back?"

She has to be able to see the answer written all over my face. I know she couldn't have missed the way I followed her every movement with my eyes. We both chuckle a little at the obvious answers as I squirt some of the liquid on my hand. I rub my hands together while she turns her body so her back is facing me. I press my hands to her back and run them along her shoulders. Something like this shouldn't feel so taboo, but I think our history makes this a sketchy area.

When I slide my hands under the strings of her top, I see the expansion of her chest with a large breath. The heat of touching her is racing through me, causing a pounding in my chest and a rerouting of my previous blood flow. I finish up and smooth the remaining lotion on my hands across my chest. She turns back towards me and we seem to stare at each other for a minute before she reaches for the lotion at my side. With a spin of her finger she motions for me to turn around so she can get mine.

I wonder if she is using her hands to talk to me because she is as worked up as I am. I wouldn't trust my voice right now to not give away how badly I want to put my hands back on her. I watch her throat as she slowly swallows and then turn so that she can return the favor. Her hands on my back are like a bolt of electricity and I love the way it seems to travel down my spine. Her soft breath lands on my neck as she works to spread the lotion on my shoulders and I know instantly that this is the most innocent and yet erotic moment of my life.

When her hands finally leave my back, I stay turned away from her long enough to not make it very obvious how her touch had affected me. I look out across the beach for a minute and try to push all of the thoughts of her skin under my hands and her touch on my back from my mind. I turn back around when I have things under control and know immediately that it won't be that way for long. She's lying back on her towel with her eyes shut behind her glasses and I follow the sun's path down her body, over the curves of her breast and lower to her flat stomach. Maybe spending a few hours at the beach with her was not the best idea.

Chapter 5

S ophie

What I thought would be a relaxing day on the beach turned into the sweetest form of torture I have felt in a very long time. Stepping off the curb in front of the hotel to see all 6'3" of solid muscle waiting for me had been so exciting it felt like a spark had ignited somewhere in my gut. He was wearing a tight fitting t-shirt that did very little to mask the lean muscles it was covering. His board shorts hung low on his hips and he must've run his fingers through his hair minutes before I'd seen him because it looked perfectly messed in a way that made my fingers itch to run through it.

He appeared not to notice the way the female population on the strand seemed to feel his presence and turn their head to watch him as he walked beside me. It was as if his piercing masculinity was calling out to their biological clocks and they were helpless to it. He was doing a number to my insides as well. Clearly every part of me was interested in every part of him and the warm tingles were everywhere making it impossible to ignore.

I was proud of myself for pulling it together by the time we had made it to a location that was far enough away from the hotel. My heart slowed down and I felt my stomach unknot with the chance of running into the girls decreasing each step we took. Of course, that relief was short-lived because Andrew had reached down and taken my hand in his as he guided me onto the sand. It was the briefest of moments, but I swear it made my insides completely melt.

I didn't think he could be any more perfect, but then he removed his shirt. I watched from behind him as his muscles pulled and flexed with the movement and I felt my mouth go completely dry. His dark tattoo was a beautiful addition to his glowing skin. I was totally staring, and not in a way that I was ever going to be able to play-off as a quick glance or accidental peek. This was full on hero worship. My skin prickled with goose bumps even though the temperature outside had to be in the high eighties. It was as if it was trying in vain to rise up and get closer to him.

I've been a good girl for a very long time. It's been helpful for me to bury myself in my work so that the pain of what Evan and Rachel had done didn't sting so much and the fear of trying to rebuild a relationship with someone else didn't seem so daunting when I didn't have time to think about it. The problem is that apparently not having a man's hands brush across my skin had made it all the more exquisite when I finally felt Andrew's on my bare back. There is no describing the way my nerves had lit up and sent pulses of electricity down my spine and across my skin.

So I laid there with my eyes closed after returning the favor of wiping sunscreen all over his broad shoulders and back because if I had left them open, I would have surely thrown myself at him. I needed to remember the purpose of being on this stupid trip and forget about the way my body hummed with an angsty energy that was begging to be released by none other that my ex-boyfriend's best friend. Yes, I was hot for the best man.

It wasn't my imagination that he kept looking at me. I would feel it like it was a physical touch, the way his eyes glided over my curves. The first few times I tuned over or adjusted my top, his eyes would fall to where the movement was and he seemed mesmerized by the small peek of new flesh that had been previously covered, or the motion of my curves as I turned to feel the heat of the sun somewhere new. Ok, so maybe I moved a little more than I would have if sunbathing with a female friend, but I couldn't help it. He had me so wound up I needed to do something to burn the energy.

After a few hours we'd packed up and headed back to the hotel. Rachel and Evan have plans for us to all have a few drinks tonight in a hotel bar so those of us who don't already know each other can get better acquainted. At first I thought drinking my way through this weekend would be the right move, but now I wonder if adding the alcohol will lower my inhibitions enough that I'm going to end up in a big heap of trouble with the best man.

I rub the lotion down my freshly shaved skin and breathe it in reminding myself that I'm almost one more day closer to returning to my predictable life in California. Tonight is supposed to be casual so I'm sliding on my favorite sundress over my matching lacey underwear. The dress is a soft lace that falls to the top of my thigh and loops around my neck in a halter style. No bra is possible since the top is more like a bikini than anything you might wear to a work meeting. A thick band of lace connects the triangles to the rest of the snug fitting fabric and a gold loop sits delicately just above each breast.

Having my skin sun-kissed is helping to make the bright teal color of the dress stand out. I have my long hair curled and pulled off my neck in a ponytail with my bangs swept to the side to soften my face. A small touch of make-up and of course the perfect shade of pink shimmer lip-gloss complete the whole look.

I stand back from the mirror to make any last minute adjustments and worry for a minute if maybe the dress is a little to revealing for a wedding event. Who am I kidding? If I had to put money on it, Rachel will be wearing less fabric than me. I slid on my silver sandals and grab my small clutch.

As I reach for the door to my hotel room, my phone chimes with a message.

Andrew: Evan has already been drinking. Thought you should know.

I stare at the screen as my heart threatens to pound so hard it might crack a rib. This will be the first time in four years that I will see him in person. Rachel of course has had his image plastered all over her Facebook page and Instagram since the moment she told me they had begun dating, so I have an idea of what he looks like now. Maybe I just need to put myself on the same playing field.

Twisting the small top of the vodka bottle is getting easier. I'm not sure that's a good thing. I tip it up and drink it down, feeling the burn drop down my throat and create a ball of heat in my stomach. If one seemed to help, maybe two would totally do the trick. It's worth a shot. By the time I finally step out of my room, my limbs are warm and relaxed and I feel a small flush of heat in my cheeks.

The bar they chose is in a hotel a small walk from the one we're staying it. I take the strand to get there and offer my ID to the bouncer at the door. I turned twenty-one a few months ago and barely even use my ID in California since going out isn't on the top of my list when I'm working long hours. The bouncer takes a little longer than necessary to make sure my picture matches my face and the last time I checked, my legs were not featured in my DMV photo. He hands it back to me with a smile and I tuck it back in my clutch.

The music is on so loud I can feel it vibrate in my body. I stand on my tiptoes so I can see over the crowd to find the wedding party. It looks like most of them are gathered around a few tables in the back corner. I drop back down flat on my feet and take a big breath before pushing my way through the mass of hot bodies to get to the corner. When I finally step out of the crowd and stand at the far outskirt of the group, my eyes meet Evans and my heart completely sinks.

I can't tell you what the feeling is. At first I thought is was longing, like my soul misses him, but then it began to feel more like regret or embarrassment. Most accurate would probably be a mixture of a few emotions and none of which feel good. His smile falls for a second and his eyes sweep over my body. I've changed in the last four years, what once was the body of a teenager is now the well taken care of body of a woman.

I take a step closer and his smile returns as he opens his arms to give me a hug. I turn my head to the side and catch a glimpse of Andrew as he looks at me over his drink. There is a warning in his eyes but I don't know if it's for me or Evan. I feel Evan's hot breath on my ear as he slurs, "Fuck Sophie, when did you grow up?" As the heat leaves his mouth and fans out across my skin it becomes ice water, chilling me down to my bones.

Rachel puts her hand on my back and Evan pulls away. Suddenly I understand the warning text and wonder when's the earliest time I'm going to be able to get out of here without seeming like a sulking child. Rachel hugs me and leads me over to where the rest of the women are standing. It looks like they might have been here for a while and I feel a little embarrassed that Rachel hadn't told me, but I don't blame her since I bailed on the afternoon of gossip at the beach today.

I stand for a minute in the circle as the women talk about their weddings and the upcoming events. Every one is trying to shout over the loud music and it makes hearing anyone more than a few inches away from me impossible. Finally when it seems like they have all fallen into a comfortable flow without me, I slip away and saddle up to the bar. It only takes a second to get the attention of the young bartender when I lean over and use my assets to speed up the service. Sometimes guys make it so easy.

"What can I get you?" His voice is deep and he has to lean across the bar and yell in my ear as the speakers above him blare the loud music.

I lean forward a little more and yell, "What do you recommend? Something sweet and girly."

"I know just what you need." The innuendo makes me giggle as he winks and pulls out a thin hurricane glass, filling it with a few different alcohols and finally some sort of pink juice. He finishes it off with two strawberries and slides it over to me. I reach into my clutch to pay, but he clamps his hand on top of mine and says, "It's on the house. Just come back to me when you're ready for another one." His smile is very charming and I blow him a kiss before sucking the magical concoction through the red straw.

I look across the bar and check on Rachel's group. They seem to be getting along just fine without me, so I sit on the bar stool and sip my drink. It's not long before I feel the presence of a large man behind me. He puts his large hand on my back and his soft lips brush against my ear. "Evan's trashed. If I were you I'd stay away from him tonight." Andrew's voice rolls through me and I might have actually closed my eyes, as his words seemed to heat up my skin.

He sits down on the stool next to me and turns so his legs are on either side of my body. "I kind of got that. Thanks," I say, turning my body towards his. I pull a strawberry from my glass and suck the pink liquid from it before taking a bite. I'd done it because it looked delicious, but seeing the way his eyes tuned dark and followed the small berry to my lips was so hot. When I licked my lips slowly it was done completely on purpose to drive him a little crazy.

His lips curved up and he took a drink of his dark colored liquor. I let my eyes move from his dark pupils to the little bit of scruff he hadn't shaved. He's wearing a black button up shirt that fit snugly and is left un-tucked from his dark jeans. I can smell his cologne again and can't resist leaning up to his ear to announce, "You smell good." When I move back to look in his eyes I can see he is pleased.

This time he leans in, "You smell like heaven and sin, but it's nothing compared to how you look tonight." I really love tipsy Andrew. I feel my skin pebble again and every part of my body that is intended for making babies tightens and aches for him. It's a heady feeling that makes my buzz so much more disorienting.

It's wildly inappropriate to be having dirty thoughts about the best man in the middle of a bar during a wedding event for my best friend, but that doesn't stop my brain. This is the most fun I've had in a long time and I'm enjoying the feeling of being desired again. Since it's so loud I mouth, "Thank you," to him to which he nods. My fingers dip into my glass again and find the second strawberry.

When I pull it from the pink liquid I hold it up to Andrew in an invitation to eat it. His smile brightens and he hesitates. I worry that maybe I'm being a little too forward, but he leans in again and his husky voice slides across my skin, "As hot as it would be to eat that strawberry from your delicate fingers, I don't want to miss the opportunity to watch your lips on it."

Now the ache I've been feeling for him seems to scream as the coil inside me grows tighter and tighter.

His hand had rested high on my thigh when he leaned in and this time he didn't move it away as we sit locked in a stare with the glistening strawberry between us. The sexual tension is so thick it could be sliced with a knife. The buzz of alcohol and the alarms ringing inside my body conspire to create a genius idea. I let my tongue lick slowly across my lips before lightly sliding it across the dark red skin of the strawberry.

Andrew watches, his breathing noticeably affected and his pupil dark with need. I encircle the red berry with my lips and then slide it slowly from my mouth with a small pop when it's finally free. I think I hear a groan, but the music is so loud it's hard to tell. I turn the berry towards his lips and they part slightly as I rub it along them. I press it into his mouth and he sinks his teeth into it, sending heat down my arm and straight to my core.

His hand on my thigh grips me a little tighter and I dip my eyes down to follow his strong arm from where his hand is pressed to me back up his body. His jeans are noticeably tighter and he doesn't shy away when he sees me looking. When I finally drag my gaze the rest of the way up his body I'm so lost in the lust between us I feel drunk. He folds the small red straw in his cup over the edge of his glass and downs the rest of his drink as if it would help to put out the fire were creating. He sets it back down on the bar and I watch as his lips part to speak but it isn't his voice I hear.

"What the fuck is going on here?" The slurred voice of my ex rings out above the loud base of the song screaming from the speakers above us.

Chapter 6

A ndrew

It takes a minute for my head to register the drunken slur behind me. The fog of desire that has been so thick between us almost makes completing any thought other than a dirty one impossible. I feel the muscles in my jaw tighten as anger pulses through my veins. I knew tonight had the potential to get ugly; I just didn't think it would happen so soon.

Giving her thigh a quick reassuring squeeze, I look into her eyes and try to express that I'll take care of this. My asshole best friend has put her through enough shit already. I have no idea how long he'd been watching us, but my guess is he'd had his eyes on her since she first walked in. I turn my head to look up at Evan, "What are you talking about?" I let my hand fall slowly from her thigh and turn my chair so my body is blocking his path to her.

Evan huffs and I can see that he is trying to think of a way to say his next words without me calling him on the hypocrisy of hooking up with your best friend's ex. I'm curious how he's going to pull this off. "Shouldn't you guys be over with the group?" His eyes shoot daggers into mine and I lift a brow at his intensity.

"She was just getting a drink, and I need a refill." I lift my empty glass so that he can see it's the truth. I can see he isn't buying it so I decide to add a little more information to sell the story. "I came over here because the bartender was laying it on pretty think with her. I saw and decided to do something about it."

His eyes soften a little as he looks between us. "Grab your drinks and come hang out with us!" He gives me one more warning glare before turning around and pushing his way back to the group.

"Oops," Sophie's voice carries over the loud beat. She shrugs her shoulders and takes a sip of her pink drink. I watch as her lips pucker around the straw and feel the fog rolling back in. Her tongue slides across her lips collecting the moisture before she says, "I guess we have to go back."

"Probably the right thing to do." It's absolutely not what I want to do though. What I want to do includes more strawberries, those pink lips of hers and my hotel room. This week is going to be torture. We stand up together in the small space between our two stools and her breasts press against my chest. I can't resist wrapping my arm around her waist and puling her a little closer.

The line about the bartender wasn't a lie. It really was the reason I was making my way over to her. I'd watched him lean across the bar further than necessary and stare at her chest while he poured her drink. It was as if someone shot me with a dart of testosterone because I couldn't get across the bar and subtly claim her in font of the douche fast enough. She has no idea how innocent she looks and how that alone would cause a flurry of dirty thoughts in men's minds.

I purposely rest my cheek against hers when I say, "Stay close to me tonight. You look fucking gorgeous. Like all kinds of sex on a stick and I want to make sure no one tries anything you don't want." Her hands grip my shirt like her knees might have gone a little weak and damn if my dick didn't enjoy that.

I start to pull my lips away from her, but she pulls me back. "Who says I don't want someone to try something?" I'm pretty sure I've descended into a circle of hell having her soft little body pressed up against mine while her ex, my best friend, is only a few feet away watching the whole thing. I know he is has no boundaries, but before this wedding I had liked knowing I had some.

"You have no idea how good that sounds," and just to reassure her I press her closer so she can feel exactly how her little show has affected me. "But you've had a lot to drink and I don't know you well enough to know if you're going to regret it in the morning or when all of the people from the wedding find out about it. Rachel's your best friend and Evan is mine. If we did anything, and God, please believe me that not doing anything is taking everything I have, I'm worried it will get out and your reputation will be drug through the gutter."

Her response surprises me. "Why couldn't it have been you?" She pulls back and looks at me. I'm not sure what she means so I pull my brows together and tip my head a bit. She smiles up at me and moves her lips back to my ear. "Why couldn't it have been you back then instead of Evan? Why didn't I see how much more of a man you are then him? It might have saved me a lot of heartache." Her words make my heart hurt.

"I asked myself that so many times back then. Why he had to find you first? In all these years I haven't been able to figure it out. I guess it's just the way it was meant to be." This time I press a small kiss to her cheek not giving a shit of Evan sees it. I might be crossing some lines with her, but the lines I'm not crossing he should be grateful for.

She steps out from our small space and I let my hand rest on her back, guiding her to the group. Rachel smiles and waves her over right away. This is how it should be. I should be with the guys and she should be with the women. I know that and I can tell myself that, but I can't stop my eyes from seeking her out and my heart from pounding when her eyes meet mine each time. I want her so bad I ache. Reminding myself that I have built a friendship with Evan for years is the only thing keeping me from throwing her over my shoulder and carrying her off to my room.

As the night goes on, she seems more comfortable with the woman and I swear Rachel can't get enough of her. The two seem inseparable again and I find myself becoming more involved with the conversations around me. The guys are talking about the bachelor party, which is going to be held at a little strip club a few blocks from here. I wonder if Rachel knows, but I doubt it. I'm about five more drinks in when Marty moves to stand beside me.

"What's the deal with Sophie? Holy shit! I swear she didn't look like that when Evan was dating her." His words are slurred and I'm sure mine would be also so I just nod my head and hope he shuts up. No such luck. "You think Evan would be cool if I try to get a little while she's here?"

"He would not be 'cool,'" my words bite and I try to keep the muscle in my jaw from ticking and giving away how badly I want to punch him.

"What's the big deal? He's getting hitched and she's fucking hot. Any guy would be stupid not to try it," I take a long sip from my strong drink trying to keep my fist occupied with something other than the need to slam right into his face. He elbows me and my drink sloshes around from the impact. "It's not like I'm the best man!" And there it is, the reason that I can't have her.

"I wouldn't even ask him. There are tons of other chicks in here right now. Go try to get it in with one of them. Stay away from Sophie." I hold up my empty glass as if to signal that it's time to refill and move away from him before I lose my restraint. I find a seat at the bar and order my drink. Spinning around on the bar stool I rest my elbows on the bar and watch the group from a safer distance.

Evan spots me alone at the bar and leaves the group to join me. He copies my position and sits quietly for a minute watching everyone drink and talk. Finally he turns his head in my direction so I can hear his voice above the music. "It's fucking driving me insane man." He scrubs a hand down his face and reaches for his drink. "The guys can't stop talking about how bad they want to fuck her and I swear I'm going to lose my shit if one of them tries." He doesn't have to tell me he's talking about Sophie and not Rachel. I know how the guys feel about Rachel and it is nowhere close to wanting to fuck her.

"They're just drunk. None of them have the balls to try. Focus on your future bride and let their drunken comments about your ex go." The bartender hands me my drink and I immediately fold the small straw over the edge. I'm drunk now for sure, not just buzzed, but full on plastered and having to listen to this shit from Evan is not making stopping any easier.

His hand claps down on my shoulder and he stands up. "You're right man. None of them have a chance with her now. Sorry about earlier, I know you are too good of a guy and a friend to try anything with her. I just wasn't thinking. Having her here is doing all kinds of shit to my head. Rachel insisted she be invited." He takes the last sip from his drink and holds it up for the bartender to see.

I don't respond to his words as he turns to face the bar and wait for his drink. Sophie and a few of the other girls are now in the center of the bar dancing to the music. I watch her dip low and roll her hips slowly as she lets her head drop back and closes her eyes. I pray that no guy gets the courage to try and touch her because I'm going to have to murder them right here in the bar. Right now I want to just sit here and imagine what it would be like if she was dancing like that for just me.

Her head lifts and her eyes, which are hazy from all the alcohol open and lock right on mine. She winks at me and then runs her hand down her body in the sexiest move I've ever seen a girl do in the middle of a dance floor in front of about fifty men that want to take her home. I'm beginning to wonder if there will be a point in this whole fucking wedding extravaganza that I won't be hard for her.

Evan's voice pulls me from my thoughts. "I'm going to head back over to the guys. Thanks for setting my head straight." He pushes off the bar and I see the exact moment his gaze lands on Sophie. "It's such a fucking tease. I wonder if she's a better lay now. Her body didn't move like that when we were younger."

I don't know if he's saying that honestly or just to try and make it clear that she's not worth going after. I nod my head but keep my eyes on her as she continues to move in perfect step with the music. I love the way she keeps bringing her yes back to mine and how a perfect blush has worked it's way across her chest and up her neck. It makes me want to taste her. I doubt that she was ever a terrible lay, but I have a feeling if she were, it had more to do with him than her.

We close down the bar around two a.m. and begin our walk back to our hotel. The strand is dark in between each of the dim lights that only illuminate a small circle of pavement. Evan can't even walk straight and has his arm slung around Rachel whose giggling like crazy. Most of the group is moving quicker than those of us in the rear and soon it's just Evan, Rachel, Sophie and I moving at a snail's pace in the darkness.

I'm looking everywhere but at Sophie, knowing that chancing a look at her could mean I'd find her staring back at me, or worse, staring up at Evan as he openly gropes Rachel and whispers loud enough for all of us to hear what his plans are for her tonight. It's disgusting. Finally we make it into the lobby and stand waiting for the elevator to pick us up. When the doors open and Evan and Rachel step in, he puts his hands on the side of her face and kisses her more passionately than

I've ever seen before. I look quickly at Sophie and see the shock and hurt on her face.

Rachel at least has the decency to look embarrassed when he finally lets her up for air. Sophie takes a step closer to getting on with them, but I reach out and grab her elbow, stopping her before she can. I shake my head and look into my best friend's eyes. "We'll catch the next one." His eyes flare with anger, but I just stare back at him so disappointed in how he's handling this whole thing.

"Thanks," Rachel calls out as the doors slide closed. We're left standing in an almost empty lobby staring at the doors because it feels too intimate to look at each other when I know how raw her emotions must be right now. It feels like an eternity has passed by the time the doors slide open again. We both step on and as the doors close I look to her expecting to see the hurt n her eyes. What I see there is something else entirely.

At this point my blood might actually be more alcohol than blood cells and all the thoughts of boundaries and bro code go flying out the window when eyes so full of need and desire are staring back at me. I close the distance between us and tangle my fingers and the smooth strands of hair pulled up on the side of her head. My lips meet hers as her hands twist in my shirt and pull me to her like I'm a lifeline and she's drowning.

A soft moan escapes her mouth and I swallow it with mine, thrusting my tongue into her mouth as she melds her body to mine. She tastes like alcohol and strawberries, sin and redemption. Her hand slips down my stomach and over my dick, and this time I groan with the contact. I kiss and suck a trail down her neck as she tips her head giving me more access. On a breathy whisper she begs, "Come to my room." There is no way I can turn that down right now. It would take divine intervention when her palm is sliding up and down over my jeans.

"Yes," I say as the elevator jumps a little when it reaches our floor. We separate just seconds before the doors slide open and a very pissed off Evan and a flustered Rachel appear right in front of us. Damn it! I didn't want to waste any time getting my lips on Sophie again. I'm not sure if Evan is pissed at Rachel or irritated that I rode up in the elevator alone with his ex.

Rachel shrugs her shoulders and reaches for her best friend's hand. "I told Evan that I wanted to have a slumber party with you tonight to catch up. Don't mind his grumpy face, he's just upset that I'll be sharing your bed instead of his." Somehow I doubted that.

Sophie looked at me quickly before stepping into the hallway and squeezing Rachel's hand. "Sure. That'd be fun."

Chapter 7

Sophie

There are so many feelings swirling around in my body right now. I'm disappointed I won't get to see where a night with Andrew will take me, but also relieved that we'll have avoided a possible awkward morning after. I feel curious and if I'm honest, suspicious about Evan's behavior. I know he isn't a big fan of Andrew and I spending time together, but I thought maybe he would see the hypocrisy in that and know to keep his opinion to himself. Instead, he looks so angry and flustered I'm a little worried he might start something with Andrew when Rachel and I are no longer around.

The boys are walking a few steps behind us as I turn towards my room. Sliding the key in the door, I open it wide for Rachel and she steps inside without so much as a look behind her. As I close the door, my eyes meet with Andrew's and I can see the disappointment in his crystal gaze. A small wink from him just before the door shuts lets me know that he isn't angry, just as frustrated as I'm feeling.

"Wow, this place is really nice," Rachel says as she makes her way to the window at the far end of the room. Her hands reach to pull the curtains back slightly so she can look out over the beach as the moon casts light down the shore.

"Yes. It's one of the nicest rooms I've stayed in. Didn't you get to preview the rooms before you had them reserve a block for your guests?"

She shakes her head as she still peers out instead of facing me. "We only looked at the honeymoon suite. I guess we didn't really think too much about other people." Her voice fades away at the end as if she might feel a small amount of regret for that. I sit down on the end of the bed so the feeling of slowly spinning can reside. I let out a small laugh without humor not thinking and quickly look to her to see if she heard me.

Her head is bowed and she has a tight grip on the curtain still in her hand. "I know you think I'm selfish Sophie." I feel my stomach knot so hard it makes me flinch. "I'm hoping one day you will truly forgive me for falling in love with him. I swear I didn't mean to."

I let myself fall back onto the bed and suck in a big breath as I wait for her to continue. She still can't look at me. "We tried hard not to. I think we both just missed you so much that it brought us together." I wonder something myself, like will my vomit actually taste like strawberries when she finally makes me throw up? "We wanted to wait until it wouldn't hurt you. You know I wouldn't do anything to hurt you on purpose." Her head finally turns in my direction, but I don't want to look at her.

"Rachel, I trust that you wouldn't have tried to hurt me." I need to. If I thought that she had made choices knowing how badly it would hurt me then our friendship would be over. I've put a lot of time into us and it breaks my heart to think that she could throw it away so easily.

"I think when you find someone for yourself it won't even matter anymore. We can both move forward without all of this between us. I can't be happy if you aren't happy for me. I know how selfish that sounds, but it's the truth. I love you." I feel the bed beside me dip as she moves to sit on the edge. She doesn't try to touch me or even force me to look her in the eyes.

"I love you too, Rachel. I'm fine, really. I'm here to watch my best friend marry the man she's in love with. That's the important thing about this week." I open my eyes and reach out my hand to hold hers. She smiles down at me and then lies back, still holding our hands between us.

"My mom wasn't happy when I told her I was going to ask you to be my maid of honor. She told me I was selfish to ask you. Her and dad act like I've committed a horrible sin dating him after the two of you were together so long. They said I'd be lucky if you even showed up." She turns her face to me and a tear falls down into the comforter below us. Reaching up with my thumb I brush away the wet trail on her cheek.

"I wouldn't have missed your wedding. I'm a big girl. I can handle this. They'll see that we can still be friends and leave you alone." I give her hand a tight squeeze. Rachel's parents have always been hard on her. They forced her into so many things as a kid. She had to be the best at everything. I know that many times they had asked her why she couldn't be more like me. She'd of course call me crying, telling me that she would never be good enough.

I never felt competitive with her. Sure we were in the same grade and I often did better in my classes, but she was a better musician and I was always envious of the way she seemed to pick up the piano as if she'd always played it. I had more success in high school, holding office in leadership and volunteering my time on the weekends to various organizations, but Rachel had also given her time to worthy causes. Where I had thought we complimented each other, at times she had felt that she had to do better so her parents would be happy. I never wanted that for us, but there was nothing I could do as a teen to stop it.

"They can't wait to see you on Thursday." She smiles at me before turning her face back to the ceiling. "Dad can't stop talking about how proud he is that you graduated from college early. I swear I could kill your mom for telling him that." She laughs and I know she's only half joking.

"It's not what you wanted Rachel. If you did, you would have been able to graduate early too. I wish you'd stop letting them push my goals on you. We're different people." I watch as she nods her head and takes a small breath.

"They really love Evan. I really love Evan." Her laugh makes me smile. I can see how much she loves him and as hard as it was for me to accept, I'm happy for her. "They were a little angry with us at first, but I knew they'd get past it. They've known Evan since you started bringing him around in high school. Dad loved talking sports with him and mom always though he was so polite." I feel my lips curl into a smile at her words. She's bringing back such sweet memories of all of us hanging out at her house after school and in the summertime. They had a pool so of course out of all the houses we could go to, theirs was first on the list on hot days.

"I'm sure once they see that you and I are fine they'll stop bringing it up to you." I don't tell her that my parents had been worried about me too. It seems that everyone could see how hard this was going to be on me but her. I appreciate everyone's concern, but I know that it's been four years since he and I broke up and surely if he had dated anyone else but her they would all be telling me to get over it instead of attacking Rachel. I actually feel bad for her. Here it is the week of her wedding and she's feeling judged by everyone.

"Thanks, Sophie. As always you're the best." We both laugh because she'd been saying that sarcastically since we were little. It became a joke between us over the years.

"You're welcome. Now get to sleep so your face isn't all puffy for your bridal shower tomorrow. What kind of maid of honor would I be if I let you show up looking like you had to fight your way there?" This earns me another laugh. She lets go of my hand and turns her whole body to face me. Extending her arm out, she invites me in for a hug. It feels good to have some of the air between us cleared.

"Goodnight." She let's me go and climbs up my bed to tuck herself in, kicking her heels off just before she pulls her feet beneath the large comforter. I follow behind her, vowing to take a shower first thing in the morning and to ask for a fresh set of sheets so I don't have to tuck myself into a bed that smells like a bar tomorrow.

I lie on my bed with a heart that feels a little lighter. What's done is done and there's no going back to change any of it. Hearing that being with my ex had been a hard choice for her was something I needed to hear. If she was willing to face all the opposition thrown her way by the people that loved us both, then maybe her love for Evan was more than my love for him had been. I know that I was never in love with him so deeply that I would have destroyed my friendship with her to keep him.

Tomorrow afternoon we're going to celebrate her new life with Evan by showering her with gifts. Both of our mother's will be there so I know that in order to make the day go beautifully for Rachel, I'll need to hold back any negative emotions until I'm alone again. She needs me to show our mothers that what she did doesn't continue to hurt me. She needs them to see that our friendship has survived and I accept that she loved him more. Maybe then we can all believe that it was them that were meant to be together forever, not he and I.

I finally close my eyes having stared up into the darkness for a long time after her breaths had evened out. I'm one day closer to being back in California with my friends. I tell myself that I'll be a different person by the time this week is through. I will have my head up again and my shoulder back, no longer weighed down by the burden of carrying this betrayal for so long by myself. When I see them vow to love each other for the rest of their lives, I can finally let go of the idea that this was just a passing thing between them that Rachel had so carelessly gambled our friendship on.

My phone chimes from my small clutch and I slip from the bed to switch it to vibrate so it doesn't wake Rachel.

Andrew: If you need help burying her body don't hesitate to wake me. I thought of a great place while plotting Evan's murder until he swore the sleepover was really Rachel's idea.

Me: Thank you. Sorry about how the night ended. Enjoy your day tomorrow.

Andrew: Nothing a cold shower couldn't fix. Paintball for the guys tomorrow. It would be impossible not to enjoy shooting some of these douches.

Me: Be careful. I think Evan was pretty pissed tonight.

Andrew: I'm not afraid of Evan. One day he'll learn that hurting people is a risky game. The consequences can be pretty high.

Me: Are we still talking about paintball?

Andrew: We could talk about something else. Like maybe what you're going to wear to bed...

Me: We wouldn't want that cold shower to have been for nothing. Goodnight.

Andrew: Too late. Goodnight and good luck tomorrow.

I switch my phone to vibrate and crawl back under the covers. I can't help the smile that stretches across my face as I picture Andrew tucked into his bed across the hall. If no one would notice, I would ditch the bridal shower tomorrow and tag along with the guys. The opportunity to shoot Evan, even if it's only with paintballs, is almost too good to pass up.

Chapter 8

Andrew

Tonight did not end the way I wanted it to at all. I wanted to take Sophie back to my room and finish what we'd started in the bar, not end up alone in my hotel room taking a cold shower. I hear my phone chime again and I reach for it with a smile on my face expecting it to be Sophie since we just said goodnight. Instead, it's a text from Evan.

Evan: I need to talk. Open your door.

Me: It's late.

Evan: Who cares? Opening your fucking door.

Me: Fine.

I throw back the covers and reach for a pair of shorts I have sitting on top of my bag. This better be important. I'm already pissed at him for the little show in the bar and I'm still not convinced he didn't have anything to do with the slumber party going on across the hall even though he swears it was all Rachel's idea.

"Come in." My voice sounds a little harsh so I try hard to tamp down some of the anger I feel towards him right now.

"Sorry. I'm just going fucking crazy and need to bounce my thoughts off someone. You're my best man. It's your duty to listen to me." He throws himself into the chair by the table and then leans forward, opening the minibar and scanning the alcohol for something to take the edge off. "What the hell? Where's the vodka?"

Shrugging, I sit back down on my bed and run a hand through my hair. "I don't know. What are you freaking out about?" His hands drop back to his lap and he leans back in the small chair.

"What if I'm making a mistake?" His words weigh my stomach down with a heavy feeling of panic.

"What do you mean?"

"What if I'm making a mistake marrying Rachel? What if I go through with this and then I'm miserable? Our parents have put a lot of money into this for us and I know they would not help me get out of it if I change my mind." He throws his head back and looks at the ceiling. His face is pinched in concentration. "I love her. I know that I love her, but I love Sophie too." His hand reaches up and rubs at his forehead like the thought is causing him physical pain.

"You don't love Sophie." I say, very certain I'm right.

"How the fuck would you know?" His head lifts up and his icy stare meets mine. "You aren't me, man. You have no idea what I'm feeling."

"I know because if you loved her you would've never hooked up with her best friend after she had only been gone a little while. She left, and you moved on like she never even mattered." I can see his jaw tick right before his face falls. I know that look. It's guilt. He tries to wipe it away with the palm of his hand but it's too late.

"Rachel was more than willing to help with the loneliness. What was I supposed to do? Sophie was in another state. I was an eighteen year-old boy. It had nothing to do with love." He pulls a small bottle of whiskey from the bar. "Don't judge me for banging her friend. You would have done the same thing if you were in my shoes."

"Fine. You were young. But now you aren't. You've been with Rachel for a long time now. Don't you think you should have figured your shit out before you asked her to marry you?" I have to tell myself this is just cold feet so I don't punch him in the face for dragging Sophie into this crazy last minute tailspin.

"I thought I was ready. I haven't cheated on her in six months. That sounds like I'm settling down right?" He's completely serious and I move to say something but he continues, "Now that I'm here and we're going out partying again I realize that maybe the last six months have just been too busy for me to try and get with other women. Tonight at the bar it felt so good to be out with the guys again. I want more nights like this. I need to be out where everyone is having fun. When Rachel and I get married, she's never going to be cool with me doing that without her."

I can't believe he's telling me this a few days before his wedding. "I think this is cold feet. Totally normal. Go back to your room and sleep the booze off. You'll wake up in the morning feeling better and happy that you're about to seal the deal with Rachel." I stand up so that he will too, but he doesn't.

"If being trashed was causing the cold feet then I would've woken up yesterday feeling secure about marrying her. I think having Sophie here has made me realize I made a huge mistake. I know you've seen how she's changed. Fuck. It's like someone is dangling a carrot right in my face."

I bite down hard to keep from saying exactly what's on my mind. "If she was the right one you would have been thinking about her instead of making wedding plans with Rachel. That ship has sailed my friend." I take a step towards my door but he doesn't budge.

"Maybe that's because when she left, she was this meek little school girl. Sure we had sex, but it was always so boring. It was like she just had to do it to keep me around. Rachel was different. It was like she had something to prove." His lip curls up on the side and I want to beat that smug look off his face.

"See, Rachel's your favorite. Now go get some sleep."

"I wonder what she's like now?" I stop dead in my tracks on the way to my room door. Circling back around, I look into his hazy eyes. He drinks the small bottle of whiskey down in one swallow and then wipes at his mouth with the back of his hand. "You can't tell me that she hasn't changed. She's fucking hot as hell. It's been four years. I bet she's learned a lot in that time."

"Evan, I'm your best friend. Listen to me when I say that you should leave that question unanswered. It's going to get you into trouble. You've caused enough problems between her and Rachel. Go back to your room and sleep this off."

His smirk diminishes and is replaced by sadness. "I made a big fucking mistake Andrew. I'm trying to tell you that I'm still in love with Sophie. She was too far away, but this week she's close. Maybe now that she's done with school she'll come back to Florida. We could have a real shot at making things work."

I move to stand right in front of him. He has to look up to see my face. "Don't be an asshole. You don't know anything about her anymore. Let her go. You crushed her four years ago when you broke up with her. Then you proceeded to sleep with her best friend and start a relationship with her. You made your choice back then. Make the best of it." It's horrible advice to give a best friend a few days before his wedding, but right now my heart is with Sophie. I don't want him anywhere near her.

He pushes up from his chair, "You're right. I made a choice back then that I thought was the best one for me at the time. I was wrong. I know that now. I just don't know what to do about it." He takes a few steps towards the door. "You're my best friend. I though maybe you could help me figure out what my next move should be before I make a bad choice worse." I feel my shoulders slump in defeat. He's right. We're supposed to be friends and I'm letting my feelings for Sophie, his ex, get in the way of my loyalty to him. As if to make me feel even more like an ass, he pats my shoulder. "Seeing you with Sophie tonight made me realize that I never really stopped loving her. It fucking hurt to watch her having fun with you. I wanted to be the one to put that look on her face."

I don't turn around when he passes me for the door. I don't think I would ever get over Sophie either, so part of me doesn't blame him for feeling torn up about shutting that door forever. He let her go to be with her best friend. That should be enough to give me the right to try and pursue something with her, but just because he made an asshole move doesn't mean that I should.

He opens the door and then turns around one last time. I turn to look at him when I don't hear the door shut. He smiles at me but it isn't a happy smile. If I had to describe it I would say it was resigned. "Do me one last favor as my best man." I nod my head, agreeing to what he asks before he even says the words. "Give me a few months to settle into my marriage before you go after her. I just don't think I can take it." I nod my head again. I've never seen him like this before and it makes me worry a little about where his head is at. "Thanks man. I knew I could count on you." The door shuts and I'm alone again.

I stand for a minute at the foot of my bed trying hard to figure out a way this could go down that no one would get hurt. I think through every angle but always come up with the same result. Someone is going to suffer. I take off my shorts and climb back into bed, my thoughts racing around as if set on fire. It's when I finally close my eyes that the most terrifying thoughts push their way to the front of my consciousness. What if she still loves him? Could I really live with myself if I was the one who talked him out of sharing his feelings with her?

I tell myself that I could forget about it, but I know that it would plague me forever. She has the right to know how he feels just in case there is a part of her that's still in love with him. Telling her is the right thing to do. I turn over and pull the covers up higher, suddenly feeling a chill at the thought of losing her before she's even mine.

Chapter 9

S ophie

My hand is aching from writing down each gift she is given as she opens them. There are so many women here at her bridal shower that I'm beginning to think I might still be here tomorrow finishing this list and then trying to unbury her from the pile of wrapping paper that is building up around her feet. I smile up at her when I hand her the next one, taking a minute to stretch my cramping fingers.

She looks beautiful in her long coral colored maxi dress. I'm sure she picked it out with today in mind. She's always been like that. She throws her hair over her shoulder and begins to read the card out loud. I watch her face light up as she lets us known that this one is from her grandmother. With a small wave she thanks her and then begins to slide the ribbon from the package.

It takes her two hours to slowly open and display each gift that was brought here for her today. By the time I stand up from the small chair I've been sitting on, my back is aching and my toes are a little numb. I pull my navy dress down a little, fixing my belt that lifted when I stretched my arms up above my head. Rachel is handed another champagne and she starts to make her way around the room thanking everyone for coming as the cake is cut and served by the staff at the hotel. I take this moment to grab my purse and head for the bathroom.

A few women are already inside so I smile as they look at me through the mirror while washing their hands. Finally I shut the door of the stall and turn my feet so it would appear that I'm using the facilities. Instead, I reach into my purse and pull out my phone. I'm hoping there is a text from Andrew, but when I pull up my messages I only find a few from my roommates and of course one from my mother who just watched me flee the front of the room. She's worried about me and I know that she thinks I'm going to crack at any moment.

Maybe if I hadn't run into Andrew I would be closer to falling apart than I am right now. It's hard to sit up there knowing that most people in the room know the story of Rachel and Evan, including my embarrassing dismissal from our relationship. I hear my mom call out my name above the stalls and have to bite my lip not to yell at her to go back to the party and leave me to pee in private.

"I'm in the middle stall mom. I'm fine and I'll be out in a minute." I pull out the seat cover from over the toilet. I can see her feet outside the door when I finally sit down. "Mom, really. Please go back to the party."

"I'm going to wait out here for you." Her feet don't move and I give up on the idea that maybe I could stay in here for a little while before heading back out with my plastered on fake smile. When I'm finished I make sure I'm smiling as I emerge from the stall and head to the sink. I can see my mother searching my face for any signs of a crack.

"Ok. Let's get back out there." I march past my mom and grab a paper towel, wiping my hands and tossing it into the trash before swinging open the bathroom door and waiting for my mother to catch up. She says nothing even though I can see that she has a million questions for me. This morning I ran to my parent's house to say hello to her and my father. She tried to ask a few questions then, but my father had told her to leave me alone.

"Are you sure you're alright?" She finally asks as I stop next to her nearly empty table.

"I'm great mom. I'm going to get back to Rachel. Make sure you come give me a hug before you leave." Reluctantly she nods and I excuse myself to go find my friend. The rest of the shower I spend helping to make sure the hotel staff knows where to put the gifts and making the trip out to the parking lot to open her mother's car so they can be loaded.

My mom finds me on the way back from my last trip out to the hot, sticky parking lot. She opens her arms and pulls me in for a big hug. In my ear she whispers, "I'm so proud of you for doing this. I know how much it has to be hurting even if you're not going to admit it. I was young once too and had my heart broken. I couldn't have done what you're doing." She places a kiss on my cheek and I close my eyes when I feel my chest constrict with the love I feel in her arms.

With a final nod she's on her way out, calling over her shoulder that she'll see me Friday evening for the big event. Just hearing that makes my stomach roll, reminding me how grateful I am that I hadn't had a chance to eat anything during the shower. When the gifts are all secure and the guests have all left, I find Rachel sitting in a chair sipping some ice water and talking with one of the bride's maids.

"Do you need me to do anything else?"

"Yes, come sit by me!" She pats the chair beside her and I fold myself into it. "Thanks so much for all your work today. I can't believe how many things I got. I'll never finish the thank you cards."

"You're welcome. I bet you got most of the stuff on your registry. I saw a few things twice." She nods her head again.

"It was definitely a great shower. A few of the girls and I are going to head over to my moms house to help organize it all and separate out the stuff I'm going to have to return. We leave the morning after the ceremony for our honeymoon and I don't want my mom's house too look like a storage locker."

"Sure. Let me run up to my room and change and then I can help." I move to stand but she shakes her head.

"No, you've done enough. Go enjoy your day. I'm sure your mom would love to spend some time with you while you're home. I'll see you at the rehearsal tonight." I don't argue with her because I think that a little break from wedding festivities before tonight is a great idea. They have it set up for this evening so that tomorrow night we can do the bachelor/bachelorette party. I have a few hours before I have to report for duty again.

After saying a quick goodbye, I head back to my room. My phone chimes in my purse and I check my messages as I close the door behind myself and I enter my room.

Andrew: I shot him a few extra times for you. Rehearsal dinner is in three hours. Want to grab an appetizer and some drinks?

I feel my smile burning my cheeks. My heart picks up the pace as I type out a reply.

Me: Sounds great! I'm ready now.

Andrew: Come over to my room.

I cross the hall and knock on his door. When it swings open I feel the air escape from my lungs. He's wet from the shower and his bare chest is still covered in small beads of water. His towel is wrapped around his hips and I can smell the fresh scent of men's soap on his moist skin.

"Hey. Let me throw on some clothes and then we can head out." I listen to his words as I watch his eyes slide down my body, taking in my cleavage and the short length of my dress before roaming down to the small window where my painted toes are peeping out from my high heels.

"Ok." I step into his room and study his tattoo that stretches from his upper chest around to cover his back. I follow the black ink as he turns from me and love the way it seems to move with the muscles of his back. I suddenly feel warm as a rush of heat surges from the tips of my toes to the top of my head. I'm grateful his back is to me so he can't see the way my body has tuned into his, heating and flushing with a need to touch him.

I stay near the small closet as he steps around the corner and out of my view. I can hear him grabbing things from his bag and the sound of a zipper closing. When he steps back into my sight again, his dark jeans are hanging deliciously from his hips and he has on a tight t-shirt that pulls at his muscles. I feel my mouth go dry when his lips curve into a smile.

"Let's head out of the area a little so we don't run into anyone." His voice is as smooth as coffee and I soak up every line of his body as I form my answer.

"Sure." I know. It's not the most eloquent thing I've ever said, but I'm staring at perfecting for goodness sakes. We make it out to his car without seeing anyone from the wedding party. He opens the door to his white Tesla and I sit down into the soft beige and black leather passenger seat.

We drive a few miles down the coastline until he pulls into the parking lot of a small restaurant. Although it looks like it's been here for a long time, I've never seen it and I grew up just a few miles from here. The hostess seats us at a small table near a large window that over looks the beach. We glance at the cocktail menu and decide on an appetizer.

"So, how was the shower?" He leans in close and rests his folded arms on the table. I can see that his face is a little bit tanner from his day in the sun. I love the way the deepening color makes his bright eyes stand out even more than they did yesterday.

"It was good. She got tons of stuff. They should be all set." I absently rub at the small angry red bump on my middle finger where my pen has been perched all day. His hand grabs mine and he runs the pad of his thumb over the bump.

"War wound?" He lets it go as the waiter appears at the edge of our table and takes our order. When he leaves, I wait for Andrew to take my hand again but he doesn't. Instead he leans back and stretches an arm out across the back of the small booth next to him.

"It'll heal. How about you, any welts?" I feel my cheeks turn red the second the words leave my mouth. If he did have welts, I didn't see them, which would have to mean they were on a part of his anatomy previously covered by his small towel. His smile is warm and knowing as he chuckles a little with my embarrassment.

"No. I'm all clear." The waiter returns with our drinks and I quickly suck some of mine down. Andrew does the same and when I look up to his face, I find him staring out at the ocean deep in thought. My stomach churns with the sudden realization that he isn't happy. Something's wrong, I can feel it in the air between us. It's almost as if he could sense my sudden panic because his eyes snap to mine and he lets his arm fall next to his body.

"What's the matter?" I ask, not really sure I want to hear his answer.

"I have to tell you something that could completely change the way this wedding is going to go down. I'm trying to figure out how to do it in a way that will minimize the collateral damage, but I'm not sure that's even possible." His features sink into a sad expression causing my heart to ache and pound erratically in my tightening chest.

"What is it?" In an attempt to lighten the mood I add, "It can't be any worse than finding out your best friend is dating your ex boyfriend. No wait, I guess finding out that they're going to get married and you're going to have to stand right next to them as the maid of honor when it happens is a little worse." I chuckle but he doesn't even crack a smile.

I keep my eyes locked on his as he takes a deep breath. He looks away from me and down to his drink for just a second and I imagine he is trying to find the courage to share with me what's on his mind. Finally he lets his eyes drift back up to mine. "How about finding out that your ex boyfriend is having second thoughts about marrying your best friend because he thinks that he's still in love with you?"

Chapter 10

A ndrew

Sophie and I are still looking into each other's eyes, my words still hanging in the air between us. I'm looking for all of the answers in her expression, but all I can see is fear and confusion. I've done my part and now it is up to her to make the next move. Evan can't say that I didn't try to open her eyes to what he was feeling about her, and I can live with myself knowing I laid it all out.

"What are you talking about?" Her voice cracks a little and she shuts her eyes for a second as she tries to compose her emotions.

"He came to my room last night after you and Rachel went in yours. Seeing you has made him realize that he has never stopped loving you. He wanted help deciding what to do about the wedding." I give my drink a small spin before taking another long sip.

"He's crazy. What's he thinking? How could he do this? She's my best friend. I don't want to be the reason her wedding gets ruined." I see her suck in breath after breath as if her body is beginning to panic with each passing second. "What am I supposed to do about it?"

"I guess that depends on how you feel about him." Her eyes, which have been flying around the table focusing on anything but mine suddenly come to a stop and flash with surprise as they meet mine.

"His decision should have nothing to do with how I feel about him. Is he even serious? What's his plan? If I say I love him he's going to cancel the wedding or leave my best friend at the alter? If I don't love him then he's going to marry her even though he's in love with someone else?" She rests her head in her hands and closes her eyes again.

"We didn't really get to that part. He doesn't know that I'm telling you any of this. I told him he was just getting cold feet and he needed to sleep it off. He was pretty drunk, but I don't think that's the reason he thinks he still loves you."

"Oh God. Oh God." She drops her hands to her lap and then shakes her head slowly looking down at the table. "I can't be a part of my best friend's broken heart. Maybe she'd deserve it, but I know exactly how it feels to be left so I could never do that to her." I start to feel a little panicked myself since she has still not shared her feeling for him.

"When he left my room he seemed resigned to going through with the wedding. I don't know if he had a back up plan or if he was even still considering sharing his feelings with you. Maybe you don't have to do anything or maybe I shouldn't have told you. I just couldn't live with myself if I held on to a secret that could change your life."

She reaches for her drink and swallows it down, placing it firmly on the table before lifting her eyes to mine. "Would it make me a terrible person if I didn't tell Rachel? Would I be a terrible person if I did? DAMNIT! There's no good ending to this!" Rubbing small circles at her temples and closes her eyes again and takes a few slow breaths.

"Stop worrying about what's best for Rachel. She didn't worry about what was best for you. Listen to your heart. If you still love him then I think you should tell him." I lean forward and pull her hand away from her temple to hold it in mine. I silently pray that she doesn't still have feelings for him. I don't want to push her, but my heart is beating so rapidly I worry it might leap from my chest.

"You're right. I need to talk to him. I don't want to pretend that this problem will work its way out. It's not fair to any of us." I squeeze her hand and feel all the hope I have leave my body. I just opened the door for her to choose him and now I'm going to watch her walk through it.

The waiter returns to the table with our food, but neither of us touch it. We just sit in silence for a few minutes. My phone buzzes in my pocket and I pull it out and read a text from Evan.

Evan: Where are you?

Me: At lunch.

Evan: Are you with her?

I take a minute to decide what to say. His words stare back at me and I hate that I have to be in the middle of something so futile. He might still love her, but that won't change the person he is. His cheating and womanizing have never been a problem in our friendship because I have never cared about any of the women until Sophie. Now I kick myself for not telling him he was being an asshole sooner.

Evan: I tried to find her. I want to talk to her, but she's not here or with the girls. Is she with you?

Me: Yes.

Evan: What the fuck?! Are you trying to hook up with her?

Rage engulfs my body, causing tension to grip every muscle. I'm doing the right thing and he is accusing me of trying to hook up with her. He, who is currently engaged and about to marry someone else.

Me: You're an asshole. I just fucking told her about your feelings for her. You're welcome.

Evan: Sorry man. What did she say?

Me: She wants to talk to you.

Evan: I can meet her tonight before the rehearsal. That's probably the only time Rachel won't notice.

Me: Fine.

Her eyes are watching me now as I type out the messages to Evan. Our food still sits in front of us untouched, but the waiter has returned with another round of our drinks. "He wants to meet up with you before the rehearsal."

"Ok." It's barely above a whisper and I can see that most of the color has left her face. She sniffs a little and I look at her more closely trying to see if tears are going to fall. I could kill Evan for putting her in this position. "Tell him to meet me in my room at 5."

"No." My voice sounds rougher than usual and she flinches slightly as it strikes her. I clear my throat and start again. "I don't think you should meet in a room. If people saw or found out it would like you were doing something behind Rachel's back. Meet him in public, but somewhere far enough away from the hotel that people won't see you." I don't tell her that I can't stand the thought of him touching her or kissing her and being in public is the only way I won't go crazy while they're meeting.

She nods her head and a tear falls down her cheek. With a small wipe of her hand she clears it as if it never happened. I see her swallow down a lump in her throat before she speaks. "How about the lifeguard tower in front of that seafood restaurant?" I nod my head and return my gaze to the dim light of my cell phone.

Me: Meet her at 5 at the lifeguard tower in front of The Crab Shack.

Evan: I could meet her in her room.

Me: No.

Evan: We should be alone.

Me: No.

Evan: Is that you or her speaking?

Me: Both. I got you your meeting. Don't hurt her anymore than you already have.

Evan: I got the message.

We only have two hours until the rehearsal dinner and I hate that any of it is going to be wasted on Evan. "Do you want to head back now so you can get ready? I can walk you down when it's time and wait if you want."

"Thank you. I don't need to get ready. I'll wait until after I see him. I think I just want to sit here a little longer if that's ok." She spins the straw in her drink before taking a sip.

"Of course." I want to ask her what she's going to tell him. I need to know if he is going to get a second chance to break her heart again. But every time I look at her I can see the stress and sadness in her eyes and it stops me from pushing the issue any further. As each minute passes, resentment towards Evan builds. "So, have you met some good friends in California?"

Her smile returns and the clenching grip my muscles have on my heart loosens ever so slightly. "Yes. I have two great roommates. We've become close friends and a few friends from work. I don't have a lot of time for socializing so right now I'm happy with the friends I've made so far."

"Sounds like you have really begun to build a life for yourself out there." I find myself wanting to know every detail of it. Where she lives. Where she works. What she does for fun.

"I love it. I'm never coming back." She giggles as the slurping sound that echoes from her glass as she finishes of the last of her drink. I make eye contact with the waiter and he nods his head, quickly rushing over with another one. She smiles at him and spins the straw again, mixing the colorful drink. "What about you? Same friends? Serious girlfriends?" I smile at how she tries to tuck that question in among the others so it seems less important than it is.

"Same friends. A few new ones, but I don't have a lot of free time either. No serious girlfriends. What about boyfriends in California?" The ice in my glass clinks together and I reach for the new one that is next to the now empty glass.

"Sadly, no." She shakes her head and I am beginning to see the effects of the alcohol on her eyes. "I haven't dated since Evan. Not on purpose, just haven't found anyone I'm really interested in. I guess dating him left a tiny scar." She holds her fingers up in front of her face to show me how small and giggles when she closes one eye and peeks at me through the small space. She's so adorable.

"That's a long time to go without a date. There's no way you haven't been asked out. You're beautiful, intelligent and hot as hell." I haven't even finished with my new drink when the waiter returns with yet another round. The slight intoxication feels good. It makes my heart ache a little less and my brain get warm with ideas of Sophie.

"I get asked out a lot. I just don't accept. What about you? Maybe not a serious girlfriend, but do you date a lot?" I shake my head a little.

"Here and there, but nothing remarkable. Mostly my friends trying to hook me up and get me laid. I guess they have decided I get a little cranky when I'm putting that part of my life off for too long." I chuckle and she adds her empty glass to the growing monument at the end of our table. Swiping up the new one she tips it in my direction.

"To being single." She taps it to mine and a little of her drink sloshes out and down my hand. I set my drink down quickly but before I can grab a napkin she pulls my hand to her mouth and licks the cold, sticky beverage from my skin. The warmth of her tongue against the cooled flash has my complete attention. My body starts to ache for her again as she swirls her tongue around my knuckle before lightly sucking the liquid into her mouth.

As if it was not the single most innocently arousing thing I've ever had a woman do to me in a restaurant, she drops my hand and returns to her drink. I lean back in my seat and make a small adjustment, hoping my shift masks the true purpose. Only I think I've made the situation worse now that her knee is situated in between my legs and I can feel the insides of our thighs resting close together. This time when the waiter returns she giggles and tells him it will be her last.

The warm buzz of the alcohol and the heat of being so close to her without being able to touch her where I want to is making my thoughts race. My eyes fall on the soft skin at her neck and I lick my bottom lip as I remember the way she tasted last night. With an internal groan I finally give up the fight and ask her what I'm dying to know. "What are you going to tell him?"

She twists her hair up and off her neck as if she'd read my earlier thought. Her eyes are serious as they look into mine and I want so badly to beg her to not let him do this to her again. Why can't she see that he doesn't deserve her? He's not even in her league. "I'm going to tell him the truth and hope for the best." Her words run together at the end of the sentence and I know that the drinks are catching up to her a little.

"What does that even mean?" I hear the desperation in my voice, but I don't let my eyes look away from hers. I can see the small shrug of her shoulders. Her cheeks are flush now from the alcohol and her lips are plump from worrying them between her teeth. I want to lean forward, wrap my fingers into her hair and pull her mouth to mine. I want to claim her so that he doesn't have a chance to break her again. The only thing stopping me is the small voice that tells me that she might still be in love with my best friend.

"It means that I'll finally get to tell him what I've been holding onto for the last four years." Of course this is when the waiter returns with our bill and asks about containers for our food. I want to scream at him to get away from our table. I don't fucking care about containers for the damn food. I care about whether or not the girl I've been in love with since I was a teenager is going to go back to my best friend. I need to know if I should have hope that this stupid doomed wedding is going to finally put an end to my obligation to stay away from the one girl who stole my heart without ever even knowing it.

The death glare I give the waiter does not go unread and he turns and leaves us alone. I open my mouth to ask my question again, but Sophie speaks instead. "Walk me there, but don't wait, ok? I think it's best if Evan and I do this alone."

Chapter 11

Sophie

I can see the dark silhouette down by the lifeguard tower on the beach in front of me. My head is still a little foggy from the earlier drinks, but seeing Evan in the distance has a very sobering effect on my body. I turn around, looking over my shoulder to get one last glance at Andrew as he walks down the barely lit strand. If he turns around I might lose my nerve to have this conversation and beg him to take me back to the safety of my hotel room. He doesn't turn around.

My sandals sink into the sand beneath my feet and I stop for a minute to take them off and dangle them from my finger. My stomach is queasy and my heart is pounding as I approach Evan. He can hear the crunch of the sand and turns around to face me as I continue to close the distance between us. Unlike at the bar, Evan smiles at me and opens his arms to invite me in for an embrace. I look back to where the lamps shine down on the strand, but can't spot Andrew in their orbs.

"Hi, Sophie." His arms wrap around me and I feel myself tense. He must sense it because he releases me and takes a small step back.

"Hey, Evan." I brush my bangs to the side and tuck them behind my ear to help keep them from blowing with the warm breeze that is drifting in from over the ocean. I can smell the salt and feel the moisture in the air around me. This time of the evening in Florida might be the only thing about this place that I will ever miss.

"Thanks for meeting me." He tucks his hands into his pockets and pulls his shoulders back preparing for my words.

"Of course." I wonder if he can see in my face how badly I have wanted to have this conversation. While I have a lot to say, I want to hear him out first. It's been four long years since I've been alone with him face-to-face and I feel like this confrontation has been a long time coming.

His right hand moves to rub the back of his neck like he always does when he's feeling nervous. I guess there are a few things that four years has not erased. I can still remember his mannerisms and feel the slight pull to reach out and to sooth him like I had done for the years we were together. Instead I curl my hand into a fist and let it stay safely at my side. He looks around for a minute before focusing on me. "Look, I know this is horrible timing. We should've had this talk years ago, but I guess I just wasn't ready." I nod my head eager to hear the rest of his thought. "I think I made a mistake.

I miss you. I know this isn't ideal and that it could really screw things up, but I need to tell you how I feel."

I shake my head and turn into the breeze again to help keep calm by letting the air sweep over my features and push back against the tears I feel burning my eyes. When I don't speak he continues. "I needed to grow up. We were just moving so fast I got scared. I'm sorry. I'm so so sorry. Can you ever forgive me?"

I turn back to his face so he can see the concern in my eyes. "What exactly are you asking my forgiveness for? Do you even know what your actions and choices have done to me? How they've changed my life?" I know he can't, but I want him to try. I need him to search his soul for the apology I deserve after giving him those precious years of my life.

"I shouldn't have broke up with you. We should've talked about it. I shouldn't have forced you to walk out of my life." His nervous rubbing has stopped and his body stands tense in front of me.

"Breaking up is part of life. It's the risk you take every time you enter into a relationship. I don't hold our break up against you." His lips curve up into a sly smile and he takes a step towards me. I instantly retreat a step away from him and watch his smile fall. "I don't hold that against you Evan, but your next move I will never understand. Of all the girls in the world, of all the women who crossed your path after you broke my heart, why did it have to be her?"

"Sophie.."

"You took something from me that you'll never be able to give back. I trusted you. Losing that was hard enough, but losing Rachel was devastating. You shattered my world and then took the one person from me that I needed to help get myself back together. You humiliated me and made my hometown too painful to return to. How could you do that if you loved me?"

"I didn't mean to. It just happened. I wasn't thinking and she was there, so close all the time." He moves towards me again and this time I put my hand up to stop him.

"It's been four years. Are you saying that you haven't been thinking for four years? Am I supposed to believe that the feelings you are claiming to have for me now have been there this whole time? Through falling in love with her to planning this elaborate wedding? Through four years of radio silence as I rebuilt my life in California? You might not have changed in four years, but I have. I'm not that naive little girl who fell in love with you. I'm a grown woman with an older and wiser heart. You will never get to do that to me again. I don't love you anymore."

I can see the surprise in his eyes. "You don't mean that. If this is about the wedding I can fix it. I've been thinking about this since the first night. I can leave now and say I've changed my mind. I won't even tell her it's because of you. Or maybe I can marry her and then just not sign the forms or something. We still have time. I can get out of this. We should be together, Sophie. We can put this behind us."

"You can't be serious. Rachel is my friend. I wouldn't do that to her even if I were in love with you—which I'm not. You haven't changed at all. You're just as selfish as the day you ended things with us. You need to figure out if getting married to Rachel is really what you want, but don't think for a second that I'm going to factor into that equation anywhere. Come Saturday, I'm getting back on that plane and flying to California where my true friends are.

"It's hard to build a life somewhere new, and it's even harder when you try to do it with a broken heart. I've done my time in this relationship hell with you and I survived. I'm not going back there. You. Can't. Hurt. Me. Anymore."

His hand encircles my wrist and he tries to pull me closer but I yank myself free. "Sophie I get that you're mad. I did a really shitty thing, but come on. You can't mean this. We aren't done. If this has anything to do with Andrew you're making a huge mistake. He's been infatuated with you since we were in high school. He only thinks he wants you so badly because he could never have you. Once you let him in he will get over you."

My stomach rolls again and I feel the bile rising up in my throat. My finger flies up and I press it pointedly into his chest. "You don't get to do this. You don't get to be a giant fucking hypocrite. You were dating my best friend before my heart even had a chance to process you being gone! You didn't just end our relationship; you lit it on fire and burned it the fuck down! How I feel about you has nothing to do with Andrew. This is just your way of not taking responsibility for the shit that you do that doesn't work out. Maybe Andrew has liked me for a long time, and maybe it won't work out between us—but at least he knows how to wait and respects the unwritten rules between friends rather you deserve that respect or not."

His voice is laced with desperation as his hand flies up to his neck again. "What am I supposed to do? I don't want you to walk away from us. I still think this is a big mistake."

"Grow up. Learn to make your decisions from a position of consideration for those who love you. I don't care if you don't want me to walk away, you don't get to dictate what I do with my life anymore. If it makes you feel any better, I thought you were making a big mistake four years ago but now I know it was fate. Marry Rachel-- or don't. It makes no difference to me. The world will keep turning and I'll keep living. Maybe my friendship with Rachel will survive you again, or maybe it won't. It doesn't matter anymore—you don't matter anymore."

He flinches like my words have physically hurt him. It's almost as if the weight that has been on my shoulders lifts and takes up residency on his. His shoulders drop and his eyes look away from mine. He opens his mouth to say something, but must think better of it. His lips pinch together and he finally looks me in the eyes again.

My voice is stronger now as I finish my thoughts. "I'm not going to tell Rachel about this conversation because it would only hurt her. There is nothing between you and I and there never will be. I'm not a threat to your relationship." Taking a few steps back, I turn and head towards the strand. His voice behind me stills my legs.

"I'm going to marry her. If I can't have you, then she's the best I can get. She loves me. She put your friendship on the line to have me. Just know that if one day you change your mind, I'll be here. I'll love you forever." He hasn't moved, but it feels like he is too close to me even at this distance. His words fall over me like ice, chilling my blood. I turn around and face him.

"Evan, that's not true. There's no way you have that much room in your small heart. It's already too full of love for yourself. I wish you the best of luck in your life, but know that I won't be stepping back into it even if hell freezes over. You made your choices, not it's time to live with them."

Chapter 12

A ndrew

I swipe my thumb across the beading condensation on the outside of my second whisky and soda. There was just no way I could stay in my room any longer wondering what was happening between Sophie and Evan. After shaving and taking hot shower, I'd put on my black slacks, crisp white collared shirt, thin black tie and my light gray sweater. I then paced my room for twenty minutes before deciding I needed to get out of there before a wore a hole in the carpet.

I've checked my phone every five minutes for the past hour, but there are no missed calls or texts from her and now my heart is pounding in my chest as thoughts of her with Evan are running through my head. I can hear the restaurant growing increasingly noisy behind me as many of the VIP wedding guests begin to fill the reserved tables. I take another sip of my drink and let the burn distract me from the maddening thoughts.

Maybe I should have said something. Would it have made any difference if I told her how I've felt about her all these years? I wonder if I should have tried to kiss her again or maybe insisted I hung out and made sure she got back to the hotel ok. I guess none of that matters now, what's done is done. I'll know from the look on Evan's face if it worked out for him. I set the empty glass back down on the bar and turn around as Evan and Rachel enter the room.

He's smiling at his friends and family, but I can see the detached look as he tries hard to pretend this is what he wants. I can't even begin to describe the weight that has lifted from my shoulders. I lean back, resting my elbows on the bar behind me and wait for her to enter before I'll take my seat at the head of the table with the bride and groom to be. Evan has his hand on Rachel's back as he glances over in my direction, the anger in his eyes is clear when they meet mine but he quickly looks away.

I feel her enter the room before I see her. The backdraft before she steps through the large arch and into the restaurant. For a moment, all the oxygen is sucked out of the room before the burning explosion of her body emerging through the doorway. God, she's beautiful. My heart stops for a moment, as time seems to stand still. Her hand is gripping a small clutch at her side, the other playing with the dangling silver earing in her ear. She has her long hair pulled up off her neck in an elegant roll and pinned at the base of her neck. It's the perfect mix of messy and meticulously placed. I love the way it allows me to see the smooth, tanned skin of her neck.

The deep blue color of her dress stands out against the olive glow of her sun-kissed skin. A lacey overlay covers the entire dress, hanging slightly longer than the layer closest to her naked flesh. It brushes across the middle of her thighs, allowing my eyes a peek at the smooth skin of the sexiest legs I've ever seen. Her heels are nude and make her legs look even longer as she stands away from the group, seeming to search their faces for one in particular.

Her eyes meet mine and I can't help the grin that curls my lips when she smiles at me from across the crowd. She begins to make her way over to me, barely dodging the arms of the familiar people who reach out to welcome her. She smiles at a few, motioning that she'll be back in a minute.

"I think you have the right idea," she says a little breathy and I can hear the nervousness in her tone. Stepping past me, she sets her clutch on the bar and holds my empty glass up to the bartender. I chuckle and spin around, resting my elbows on the bar again. The bartender places a new drink in front of me and one in front of Sophie. She takes a big sip, and then sets it on the bar with a sigh of pleasure that has my body at attention again.

I want to ask her how it went. I need to know what happened and if I now have the green light to make her mine. I run my finger around the rim of my glass as she takes another drink of hers, never opening her eyes as if it's the most delicious thing she's ever had cross her tongue. I can't take my eyes off of her. I lean in, letting my lips brush her ear very lightly. "You have no idea how gorgeous you are. I could stay right here and watch you all night."

I see the small flush rise from her neck up to her cheeks when I back away just enough to get another good look at her. She lets out a small breath but keeps her eyes closed. I know her nerves must be shot after the conversation with Evan and having to be here tonight. I lean back in again, this time wrapping my arm around her waist and pulling her into me again. "I've been going crazy since I left you on that beach." Now I close my eyes, mustering all the courage I can to tell her what I need to. "Tell me he lost you. Tell me he was too late because I don't think I can spend one more night this close to you with out making you mine."

Opening my eyes again, I move back, watching closely as her eyes open and turn to mine. Her voice is intoxicating as she turns and presses herself against me so she can reach my ear. The heat of her breath across my skin has me so revved up I want to beg her to forget the dinner and come up to my room with me right now. Her hand grips my bicep as she whispers, "He was too late. It seems I've moved on to bigger and better adventures." She moves her face back for just a second and I turn my head to look into her eyes. That's the best news I've ever heard. Her hand on my arm pulls me back against her. "Would you be interested in that?"

She's teasing now, her arm gently stroking up mine until it is wrapped around my neck.

"I've been interested in that—in you--since I first saw you. You've been the woman of my dreams and in my dreams since I was a teenager. I just want to make sure you're ok with what might happen if Rachel and Evan find out." I hate to remind her, but right now we are pushing the boundaries in front of a few mutual friends and I know that pushing it any further in public is going to lead to stares and raised brows.

"I don't want to take any attention away from the bride." I feel her arm slide from my neck as she puts a little space between us. With a quick look over her shoulder, she surveys the room for any sign that we've been obvious. I love that she was so lost in me that she hadn't seemed to notice the other people.

"Unless you plan on leaving the room, I don't think you can be successful at that sweetheart. You'll always take the attention off Rachel when you're around." I'm rewarded with a small smile and it warms me deep inside. I offer her my arm and she takes it. I lead us over to the group and I feel her hand leave as various people come up to greet us. I feel the loss of her immediately even though she is still close. I want her with me no matter what the consequences are. If Evan is a true friend, he will want me to be happy even if that means I date her. If he can't accept it then I guess our friendship has had a good run, because she's my future.

When the hostess finally announces it's time to get started, I find my place setting and feel such relief when I see that Sophie will be beside me. I watch as she glances down the table, searching for her name card and raising her smiling face to mine when she sees where it's placed. I pull her chair out and she sits, scooting a little closer to my seat as she moves hers closer to the table.

We are offered our choice of three meals and the wine begins to flow. I notice she's taking it easy now on the wine, mostly cradling it in her hand as she chats with a few of the women around us. I'm trying not to be obvious as I sneak a glance at her every so often. When our salads arrive, the table quiets down and I can't take not touching her any longer. I slip my hand under the table and rest it on her bare knee. No one will be able to now it's there except the two of us, and it seems like the perfect solution to my need to have her skin on mine.

Sophie doesn't acknowledge it, playing into my game of being stealth. Conversation begins to pick up again as people finish their salads and the wine continues to be poured, creating a buzz for a lot of the people around us. When she lifts her glass to her lips again, I slip my hand up a little higher on her thigh. She pauses for a second with the glass resting on her perfectly plump lower lip and I know that my touch is most definitely affecting her. I love it.

We don't talk to each other the entire time we are seated at the table. I catch a glimpse of Evan watching us every so often, but I don't let on that anything is happening. Instead, I wait for a moment where she isn't wrapped up in another person and I slip my fingers softly along her inner thigh, slowly advancing my position on her leg. I'm beginning to think I have the upper hand until she laughs at something another guest has said and sets her hand high on my thigh, squeezing for a second before letting it climb higher and dangerously close to the center of my lap.

We are served dinner, but I barely pay attention to it. I can't focus on anything anyone is saying, my attention completely on the way her warm and slightly gripping hand feels on me. It's sending heat up my leg and to the part of my body that has been aching for her all night. It's a dangerous game we're playing, but I couldn't stop it if I tried. The truth is I wouldn't want to. Just when I think I can't take it any longer, Rachel announces we'll be moving out onto the beach to go through the ceremony quickly for practice.

I don't want to let her go. It's the most primal of all feelings, a deep need to touch her and make sure she knows just how badly I want her. I don't think I've ever been so turned on by just a hand on my thigh. I know it's more than that. It's her voice, her laugh, her scent and the way the air between us seems charged with an energy that's almost visible.

As everyone begins to file out into the hotel lobby I strengthen my hold on her thigh, signaling to her not to move. She doesn't fight it, just plays with her glass as if she needs to finish the last sip. When I'm sure enough people have left and the attention is no longer on either of us, I lean into her and let my hand move the last few inches until I can feel the lace of her panties with my finger. "Stay with me tonight."

Chapter 13

Sophie

The air is still warm as it whips across my skin, bringing with it the smell of salt. I tuck a small strand of hair that has escaped behind my ear to keep it from blowing in my face as the preacher goes quickly through an outline of what will take place on the real wedding day. I chance another glance at Andrew and see him watching me, his eyes never shying away regardless of who might catch him looking. My skin heats up again with thoughts of his touch.

Of course I agreed to stay with him tonight. Now I just have to get through this practice and back up to his room before I overheat and pass out from excitement alone. His lips curl up and I wonder if he's thinking the same thing as me. Clapping pulls me from my thoughts and I quickly catch up, making sure to focus my attention back on the bride. She looks so happy standing with Evan and for the first time since arriving I'm actually feeling happy for her.

Evan and Rachel turn to face their audience and begin the walk from the alter to the back of the chairs. He holds her hand and tugs her along, not once making eye contact with me. I think that's for the best. I take a few steps up to meet my escort down the aisle and allow my eyes to sweep up his fitted black slacks and along the hard silhouette of his broad chest. When my eyes meet his he leans in and whispers, "That was torture. How much longer until you're mine?" I feel my cheeks turn pink and tuck my head to hide my reaction from the audience. With a wink, he offers me his arm and I tuck my hand into the curve and let him lead me past the small audience.

My heart is beating so quickly I can feel my pulse in my neck. I catch the scent of his cologne as it mixes with the salty smell of the breeze and it fills my lungs causing warmth to spread through me. I can feel the pull and flex of his muscles under my palm and I love that even in my heels he's tall enough that I have to look up to catch him looking down at me. His jaw is flexed and the smooth, freshly shaved skin looks so heavenly I want to slide my lips across it.

"I'm so excited! It's almost time for the real deal!" Rachel's voice pierces my trance and I shake off the haze of lust that was clouding my thoughts. Her hand encircles my free wrist and she pulls me into her chest in a too tight squeeze. Suddenly we are bouncing as she jumps up and down in the sand.

"It's going to be perfect," I answer with the tiny breath of air she hasn't forced from my lungs. I love her. Even through my broken heart, I'd never given up on our friendship. I wrap my arms around her and let myself feel hopeful that one day things will be like they were before. When she finally releases me, I turn back to Andrew. His chin is tucked down and he is peering at me from beneath his dark lashes. His hands are tucked into his pockets and in this moment he's the sexiest vision I've ever seen.

"We're all going to go out for drinks." Evan's voice behind me causes my back to stiffen. Andrew's eyes flick up from mine and his smile drops. I hate that I have anything to do with the growing tension between them. Andrew has done nothing wrong; in fact, he tried hard to make sure I knew how his best friend felt about me. There is harshness in Evan's tone that almost brings down the butterflies that have been circling in my stomach with the dirty thoughts of my night to come.

"Where?" Andrew asks with a smile I know is forced.

"Cocktails. They have pitcher's of margaritas and a DJ." Evan answers before turning back to the rest of the bridal party.

I know that Andrew is doing me a favor by not walking right next to me as the group migrates down the strand towards the bar not far from our hotel. I can hear the music when we get close and I wonder how long it will take before we can slip out unnoticed by the others. He may not be right next to me, but he's ever present in my thoughts.

The bar is crowded for a weeknight. The dance floor is packed with young men and women, grinding and moving together in a way that feels both sexy and illicit to watch. I take a seat at a tall tabletop and watch as Andrew takes one a few chairs down and across from me. One of Rachel's bridesmaids sits down next to him, batting her eyelashes and leaning in a little further than necessary to reach for a margarita glass. I feel jealousy hit me like a hot spear to my gut. I also feel my phone vibrate from inside my clutch. I take my eyes off the woman and see Andrew's face. His brow is raised and he has a small smirk on his face.

Andrew: You didn't answer my question. How long before we can get out of here and away from sloppy over here?

I smile at his text and look up again. This time he's holding his hands together as if he's praying and his bottom lip is tucked so sexily between his teeth. I wonder if anyone would notice if I climbed up on this table and crawled my way across to him. I know we need to hang out for at least an hour so that there's a possibility people will be buzzed enough to not notice our disappearance.

Me: Hour?

Andrew: No fucking way. I can't take an hour. Did you even look in the mirror? You're lucky I'm a gentleman—you look good enough to eat.

Me: Thank you. If you like the dress you should see what I have on underneath it.

Andrew: Are you trying to see how long it takes me to throw you over my shoulder and leave this bar caveman style?

I laugh again and this time when I look up I notice the annoyed look on the bridesmaid's face. I guess she isn't very happy with his attention being on his phone instead of her. Her face lights up again when the third pitcher of margaritas is set on the table. I put my phone on my lap and suck the sweet and sour liquid through the straw, taking a second to lick a small trail along the rim of my glass to taste the salt before taking another sip.

Andrew: So sexy. I need to touch you. Follow my lead.

I feel the hot rush of the alcohol as it pulses through my veins and I feel my eyes grow hazy. Andrew is looking at me with such intensity it feels like he could actually scorch my skin. Forget about butterflies, there are birds in flight in my stomach and I squeeze my legs together as the heat of his gaze makes me ache for him. He doesn't turn around right away, looking at me as he takes a few steps back and towards the crowd of people dancing. When he reaches the outer edge of dancers he turns and I lose sight of him within the writhing bodies.

Glancing around the table, I see that no one is really paying attention now that the drinks are flowing and the music is flooding through the speakers making the chatting guests have to huddle around each other in order to hear. I slip from my chair and enter the moving ocean of bodies. I'm searching, but I can't seem to find him in the crowd. When I'm about to give up, I feel hands on my hips from behind. I can smell his familiar cologne and feel a slight pinch of his fingers as he pulls me back against his hard chest.

"How was that salt, sweetheart?" His voice is gravely as his breath whispers across my ear and down my neck. "First the strawberry and now the salt. That mouth of yours is driving me mad. I want to feel it on me." I close my eyes and mold my body to his, moving with the music as I lift my arms and wrap them around his neck.

His hands slide down from my hips and I feel his fingers on my thighs just past where the lace falls against my skin. Slowly he begins to pull the hem of my dress up so his fingers can seer a burning trail up my thighs. I arch my back slightly, letting my ass press into his groin and can feel the evidence of his excitement as I grind against him. With this, his hands abandon my thighs and move up to my waist, spanning out on my abdomen and moving up until they rest just under my breasts, his fingers resting on the curve teasing, but not crossing the line.

I'm so glad I decided to pull my hair up because his lips brush against my bare neck and down my shoulder. When he moves them back up to my ear, he alternates small kisses and gentle nips until I feel weak and drunk on lust. I tip my head to the side so he can lick across the soft skin. A little moan escapes my lips and I hear the hiss of his breath behind me before his hands are back on my hips, spinning me around to face him.

With out any care for who might see us, he wraps one hand around the back of my neck, tangling his fingers into my hair. He pulls me to his mouth and I go willingly, needing his mouth on mine like I need air to breathe. His tongue slides along my bottom lip before lightly entering my mouth, coaxing my own tongue out to play. He tastes like tequila and salt, the best combination for making a tingling energy gather at my core. I want this man so bad I'm aching.

His hand at my hip moves down to my ass and he cups me and pulls higher as he parts my legs with one of his own. I feel the heavy fabric of his slacks as it brushes the inside of my thighs when my hips move closer to him. My dress hikes up, allowing me to get close enough that I feel his thigh rub gently against my core. I suck in a breath at the contact and he stills when my hands twist into his sweater to pull him to me like a lifeline.

I have never felt like this before about a man. I might have loved Evan, but he never got me this worked up. All thoughts of being seen by the others in the bridal party have left my brain. All I can think about his how badly I want to explore his body with my hands and tongue. I want to see his muscles flexing over me and smell his delicious scent as I bury my face in his neck.

His hand leaves the back of my neck and I feel his fingertips at the hem of my skirt again. I pull my face away from his enough that he can surely see the need I'm feeling for him in my eyes. My bottom lip is so tightly gripped by my teeth that I wonder if I'm going to taste the slight coppery taste of blood soon. His eyes are just as needy as mine, slightly hooded with desire as he watches me react to the feel of his rough fingertips brushing under my dress hem and slowly moving to my panties.

The bar is dark and the dancers are all so close to us that it's actually proving the perfect amount of privacy. He's waiting for me to tell him to stop, but I can't. My brain is flooded with euphoria as he builds my desire with each inch his fingers conquer. As the music pulses and vibrates around us, the fingers of his right hand move to my core, lightly brushing the outside of my lacey panties, shooting a jolt of pleasure through my body that has my head falling back.

Just as quickly as they stroked across me, they're gone and his lips are back on my neck, this time a little rougher and full of hunger. I tip my head up again and lick and suck my way up his neck to his ear. I love the moan of his pleasure as I taste his skin and feel the beat of his heart in his neck. He wants this as bad as I do and that's a very intoxicating thought. When I finally reach his ear, he's grinding against me, helpless to relieve the building sexual tension in this very public place. "Take me to your room."

Chapter 14

Andrew

This might just be the best night of my entire life. Her toned body is rubbing up against me and I can feel how badly she wants this. I smile and nod my head before kissing her neck again and work my way back up to her ear. "Get your purse and meet me outside. I'll leave first and try not to let anyone see me go. You get out of here as soon as you can and meet me outside." She is already nodding her agreement and I suck the silky skin of her neck into my mouth one last time before leaving her on the dance floor.

I spot Evan at the bar with a few of the guys and he shoots me an angry look when our eyes meet. I hold my phone up and give him a look I hope he will buy as me needing to take a call outside. His small nod is all I get and it's good enough. I'm not letting him stop me right now. All that matters is getting Sophie back to my room like she asked. If I can't pick up where we left off on the dance floor, I might be the first man to actually die from the pent up sexual tension.

The air is refreshing as I wait for the door to open and deliver my girl. When she finally emerges, I feel a rush of relief and reach for her hand. I know that she needs to walk slower than I do because of the heels, but I can't help but pull her along, urging her to get back to the hotel as quickly as possible. I'm at the edge of my restraint and I'm feeling it slip with each minute her hand is in mine.

We finally step into the hotel lobby and I press the button for our floor, not looking at her for fear that I will forget all about being in public and let my needs take over no matter what the consequence is. The elevator dings and the doors slide open. Much to our credit, she and I step in calmly like any other couple returning from a small walk along the strand. As soon as they slide closed again I turn to her and put both hands on the side of her face, holding her as I press my lips to hers, tasting the salt and margarita. Her hands grip my forearms and she opens her lips inviting me into her mouth with a small pass of her tongue against my lips.

We are breathing heavy and holding on to each other as if letting go would mean the end of all of this. The elevator stops at our floor and we pull away from each other as the doors open. I'm so thankful that there's no one waiting for it because it's so obvious what we've been doing. Her hair is looser now, random soft strands framing her flushed cheeks and bright eyes. Her lips are swollen from our kisses and her chest is rising and falling quickly. I know I must look as disheveled as she does and I make a small adjustment to making the walk to my room bearable.

I pull my wallet from my back pocket and find the room key. She stands behind me as I unlock the door and I can feel the energy radiating off of her and bringing every nerve ending in my body to life with the thrill of having this reaction from her. She wants me badly, but nowhere near as badly as I want her. It's just not possible since I've had years to fantasize about what this moment might be like and now that I know what she tastes like and how her hot skin feels beneath my touch I know reality is going to completely demolish everything I've done with her in my head.

I swing the door open and hold it for her, loving the shy grin that is curling at her lips as she looks up at me. Spinning around and walking into the room backwards so that she can keep her eyes on me, she kicks off her heels one step at a time and I close the door and flip the latch wanting to be sure nothing is going to stop the forward momentum we have going right now. I need this. I need her.

She crooks her finger at me and beckons me to her causing my pants to grow increasingly tighter as every once of blood I have seems to be rushing to the same aching place. Reaching out, I capture her wrist and pull her against me, burying my head in the crook of her neck, breathing her in as I find the zipper on the back of her dress. I slide it down as I suck lightly on her skin, losing my breath when her hand brushes down my stomach and grips me through my pants. "Fuck," is all I can manage as she begins to slowly stroke me through my pants.

I run my hands up her back to the top of her dress and part it with my fingers, purposely letting them dance across her back until I see the goose bumps run down her neck and arms. Yes, two can play at this game. I slide the dress from her shoulders letting it pool at her feet. She wasn't kidding. Her breasts are full and heavy in the thin red lacy cups of her bra. Her panties ride low across her hips in the tiniest of triangles that I know leads straight to a G-string behind her. She knows I love the dress, but was so right to assume I'd love what she had on beneath it.

I don't know where I want to put my hands. I want to feel it all, taste it all, but I don't know where to start. I tuck my fingers into the waistband of her panties, but she shakes her head and begins to pull my sweater up my body. I reluctantly release her and help to pull my sweater off before reaching for my tie, not bothering to untie it, only making it loose enough to get it over my head.

I don't let my eyes leave her body for even a second as I start to unbutton my shirt. Her hand is rubbing me into a frenzy, my fingers slipping from the buttons as she tugs my belt through the loops and then slowly slides my zipper down and pushes my pants off my hips. She rolls up on the balls of her feet and tangles her hands into my hair, pulling my mouth to hers and diving right back in where we left off in the elevator. My brain completely forgets what I'm doing and I wrap my arms around her waist, needing to feel her breast against me.

I haven't been this turned on from kissing a girl since I was a teen. The small whimpers from her are ramping up the throbbing in my boxers and I press against her needing a little relief. Her hands leave my hair and grab onto my collar. Instead of working each button through its hole, she pulls my shirt apart quickly sending little buttons flying in every direction. I couldn't be more grateful for her urgency. The softness of her hands exploring my chest and abs is the most erotic sensation and I shrug the shirt off my shoulders. Toeing my shoes off and then finally stepping out of my shoes and breaking our kiss long enough to remove my socks.

Instantly my hands are back on her, expertly unclasping her bra and pulling it away from her chest. Loving that her breasts are bared to me, I let my palms softly run up her stomach before filling them with the perfect curves. A low moan escapes her lips and I quickly cover her mouth swallowing down any sounds she makes. I let my thumbs brush lightly across the tips before sliding my hands back down her body so I can tuck my fingers beneath the waist of her bright red panties. As much as I love this pair, I want to make sure I'm the last man to see her in them. I rip the band with just a slight pull and toss them to the side.

The only barrier between us now is the thin fabric of my boxers. Her hands sweep down my stomach and her thumbs tuck under the elastic band, pulling them down to my thighs so that they'll drop to my feet, freeing my very ready erection. Her lips press to my neck and she trails warm, moist kisses down my chest. I suddenly remember I need to get a condom out of my wallet. "Condom," is all I can manage and she lets her tongue circle my nipple before pulling away. "My wallet."

I can't even make a complete sentence. She laughs softly and pulls my wallet from the pocket of my pants and hands it to me. I open it but I'm quickly overwhelmed with sensation to focus on finding the foil package. Her warm wet mouth is now wrapped around me and I feel the pleasure tear through me and race up my spine. My head rolls back as she slides her mouth up and down. I feel the faintest sensation of teeth as she moves to the tip and then pulls me back in all the way down to the base.

If this goes on any longer the night is going to be over before it even starts. I find the condom and toss my wallet onto the dresser. Ripping open the package quickly, I use my free hand to pull her up before sliding the condom onto my dick. Sophie moves back towards the bed and I motion with my head for her to climb on, finding myself stalking up towards her as she crawls backward towards the headboard.

I stop when my face is between her legs and kiss her just on the inside of her knee. Her legs fall further apart as I continue my kisses up the inside of her thigh until I finally reach her center. She's holding her breath as I let my tongue lick across her core and within minutes she pulling me up on top of her. "Please." It's a whisper but it rings loudly through my body and speaks directly to a primal urge inside me. I position myself between her legs and groan when her hand grips me firmly to guide me to her entrance.

All the years of thinking about her, dreaming about what it would be like to be here with her like I am now doesn't come close to the way it feels when I finally sink deep inside her. Her legs wrap around my waist and she tangles her hands in my hair again, pulling my mouth to hers. I need to move again, but I give her a minute to adjust to me before beginning a slow steady rocking that has her clawing at my back and whispering my name in my ear.

I can feel her tightening around me and I increase my pace, reaching between us to slowly circle the small bundle of nerves at her core. I feel my orgasm building as she meets my thrusts with her own. This is by far the best sex of my life, and we are not even in some crazy position or partners that have been together long enough to know exactly what gets each other off. That's the most amazing thing about this—if it's this great now it will be phenomenal in the future.

"Andrew," her voice sends chills down my spine, winding that pleasure feeling tighter until I'm about to explode. I feel her come undone around me and press deep inside her one last time before finding my own release, chanting her name softly as wave after wave of euphoria crashes through my body. I'm ruined in this moment, completely owned by this woman I barely have my hands around. As I kiss her lips tenderly I wonder if her world has just been turned upside down like mine and despite that, when we can do this again.

Chapter 15

Sophie

I wake up wrapped in his arms when the light shines through a small crack in the curtains. I was worried that I might wake up today feeling a little regret for sneaking off with him last night when I should have been hanging out with Rachel, but I can't seem to find it in me to feel anything other than content—happy even. Last night was wonderful and I wouldn't take it back for any price.

"Good morning," his grumbly voice says from behind me, and his arm that is snaked between my breasts cinches tighter, pulling me back even closer to him. He presses a kiss to my shoulder before letting his head fall back onto his pillow.

"Good morning," I sigh.

"What's on your agenda today?"

"Nothing until the bachelorette party tonight. I can't believe tomorrow is the big day. I thought this week would never end." I laugh softly. His lips are on my skin again and I can feel them smile at my admission.

"No kidding. A whole fucking week to celebrate seems a bit indulgent." He rolls onto his back and I follow, wiggling around until my head is rested on his arm. "Can I take you to breakfast?"

"That would be awesome. I didn't really eat much last night since I was so worried about meeting up with Evan." I reach for the hand of the arm I'm laying on and pull it over my chest. I can't help feeling safe and happy wrapped up in his warmth.

"I'm trying really hard to mind my own business, but I would really love to hear what you guys had to say to each other. I could see on his face last night that things obviously didn't go the way he wanted." His lips drift to the top of my head. This feels so familiar. It's like this is the way it was always supposed to be.

"He's such an ass." Andrew's chuckle makes me smile.

"Tell me something I don't already know."

"Ok, he said he still loves me and that he will be waiting for me. He offered to call of the wedding. When I told him I wasn't going back to him, he told me that he would always be waiting. Basically, when I was ready to love him again, he would leave her. I can't believe I ever trusted him." That was the hardest part. I had trusted him. When he broke up with me it rocked that security, but when he started dating Rachel it made me doubt all of his feelings for me and even our history. He'll never know how much it scarred me.

"What?" I feel his head shaking. "Sometimes I have no idea who he is anymore." I know that feeling very well.

"Well, I guess it doesn't matter. I told him I was here for Rachel and that I would never be stepping back into his life."

"Are you going to tell Rachel about it?" His arm around me tightens a little with his words.

"She wouldn't believe me. I love Rachel, but she's always been in some one-sided competition with me. I want to believe that she fell for Evan because that's what her heart truly wanted more than anything, but I've also wondered if it had anything to do with trying to be better than me. If I told her what he said, I would lose her friendship and she would have a little seed of doubt in her about their relationship and I know how horribly tight that sprouted seed can wrap it's roots around your heart and head. I've been there." He kisses my head again letting out a big sigh when his lips leave my head.

"She'll figure it out soon enough. You don't owe her any-thing. If she can't see him for who he is then maybe she'll live in a wonderful marriage built on blissful ignorance." I can't help but laugh a little at his morbid yet adorable view of their future marriage.

"That's terrible."

"Yes it is, but it's also true. Some people filter out the information they don't want to accept. Even when it's been right in front of their face the whole time, they just choose not to acknowledge it." His words make me wonder if he is speaking from experience.

"Well," I say, rolling towards him and letting my arm drape across his stomach, "I don't ever want to be that person. Let's stop talking about this depressing topic and go get breakfast. I'm starving." I love the way his lips curl into a smile before he kisses my forehead.

I quickly gather up my outfit from last night and decide to just borrow a towel to wrap around my body when I do my walk of shame across the hall. When I know the coast is clear I run across, quickly unlocking the door and jumping inside completely undetected by the other guests. This fling has really made this week exciting. I thought I'd be spending most of it in my room sulking, but instead I feel exhilarated.

I shower and blow dry my hair and then put on just a touch of make-up since I know tonight I will be wearing more than usual for the party. My face needs a little rest from all the humidity and pore clogging make-up. I slip on a loose fitting cotton skirt that falls to the top of my knees and thin tank top that also hangs loosely giving it a very comfy, summery look. I finish it all of with my delicately beaded sandals. I grab my phone to send Andrew a text.

Me: I'm ready.

Andrew: Do you want to meet outside the lobby so no one will see us? I'd hate for the girls to give you hell tonight at the party.

Me: Good idea. I'll see you in a few minutes.

I hear his door across the hall open and then click closed before his footsteps fall onto the thick carpet outside our rooms. My stomach tightens with the anticipation of spending more time with him. I never thought I wouldn't want this week to end, but now I'm a little sad to know I only have two more days with him. Then what? He lives here and my life is in California.

When I'm sure it's clear, I step out of my room and make my way down to the lobby. The big glass doors slide open after my short elevator ride and the wave of humidity hits me again, almost sucking the breath right out of me. It's just another reminder of how much more I love my life in California. I wonder if he's ever been. Turning, my heart rushes into a sprint as my eyes find him sitting on the small wall outside the hotel.

His smile is bright and mischievous as he lets his eyes roam down my body, effectively heating up every inch of my skin even though he's nowhere near me. I should fix that. Taking a few steps, I stand in front of him and look down on his perfect face. I love that he didn't shave this morning and his jaw is lightly shaded with stubble. His hands reach out and rest on the back of my legs, pulling me a little closer so that I am sandwiched between his thighs.

"Ready, sweetheart?" I can only nod my head at his words because my brain is firing off signals to every inch of my skin. It's as if the heat of his palms has crawled up my body.

Once in his car, he leaves the beach area and drives us along the highway back in the area of my parent's house. We take the exit three ramps before my hometown and my curiosity starts to grow as he weaves us through a small residential area. The lawns are all green and the houses are stunningly beautiful. He pulls into the driveway of a large two-story home and reaches for a button on his visor. The garage begins to open, revealing a street bike and a few large toolboxes.

We park inside the garage and the large door begins to close behind us. Clearly this is his place. "What happened to breakfast?" I joke as he opens the door that leads from the garage to the house.

"This is my favorite breakfast spot." He winks at me and slides his hand into mine, guiding me inside and down a long hallway. The house is amazing. It's all dark wood and grey tones, which fit him perfectly. It's very clean and I wonder if he has roommates of maybe a maid, but the house is completely quiet.

"Do you have roommates?" I ask when he stops us in the large kitchen that proudly boasts a Viking stove.

"No. This is all mine. I don't really enjoy the frat boy life style." I laugh and move towards the counter to run my hand along the beautiful granite counter top. He walks up behind me and rests his hands on my waist, kissing my bare shoulder before spinning me around to face him.

"Your house is really nice." My voice sounds a little breathy and I tip my head to the side when his lips find their way to my neck. I close my eyes and take in the sensation, loving the way it fuels the fire that's burning inside me. Too soon, his lips leave my neck and he puts some space between us.

"Thank you. I feel like it's missing something though." He looks around the room and shrugs before smiling back at me. "Stay right here. I'll make us some food." His hands grip me tighter as he lifts me onto the counter.

"I can help," I offer, but secretly hope he doesn't take me up on it. He's already digging around for his pots and pan and I'm enjoying the view of his muscles flexing and pulling his shirt tight across his back.

"No. Sit there and tell me all about California." His voice echoes out of the cabinet he is searching in.

"Have you ever been?"

"Actually, I'm there all the time." He looks back at me over his shoulder and winks. "My firm has an office there. Sometimes I'm stuck there a few months out of the year." My head spins a little with this news and I wonder if we have ever come close to our paths crossing. "I um, I thought about looking you up a few times actually." He turns around and leans back against the counter. I'm a little speechless. "I wasn't sure if you would be happy about that so I never could work up enough courage to do it." That warms my heart so deeply I feel the tears stinging the back of my eyes.

I always thought everyone had forgotten about me. It felt so cold and lonely to leave my hometown and start over somewhere new. I would've loved for him to find me and come for a visit. Just someone familiar and friendly. "I would've loved that." He smiles again and looks down to the floor. "You should have found the courage."

His eyes meet mine again but his smile is gone. He shakes his head a little. "Even if I had found the courage, I wouldn't have trusted myself." I feel my brows pull together in question. "I've been in love with you since we were just teenagers. I always thought it was just a crush, but I know now how wrong I was. You stole my heart that first time you walked through the door with Evan. I haven't found a woman that compares to you since then. I guess I was a little afraid that I wouldn't be able to just be friends with you and you wouldn't be interested in anything more." Now his lips curl a little, but I can see the weight of his words still between us.

He takes a minute to look out the kitchen window as I sit just staring at him, unsure of what I should say. His eyes meet mine again, "I've waited a long time to make sure you were ready. I wanted to give you time to get over what he did to you. I know that being his best friend would have made me an enemy just by association. Every time I thought about reaching out, I would get this sickening thought that contact from me might make you hurt and I couldn't do that to you."

I can feel my heart swelling in my chest and I can't help but fall in love with him as he shares this with me. All that time I thought I was forgotten. And all that time he was thinking about me. Not just because my break-up with Evan was the gossip of the week, but also because he truly cared about me. I feel a tear slip down my check and his face flashes with worry as he makes his way across the kitchen.

I close my eyes when his thumb swipes it from my cheek and then his hands hold my head and tip my face up to his. "I'm sorry," he whispers. I try to shake my head and laugh.

"These are happy tears," I manage as a few more escape. His smile is warm and inviting as he pulls me a little closer and kisses me tenderly.

"Does this mean I have a chance?" He asks in between our lips meeting each other's. I nod my head and wrap my arms around him.

"You should be warned that Evan and Rachel really did a number on me. I haven't dated in four years because I don't trust anyone. I know it isn't healthy and I promise I'll work on that, but please don't hurt me like he did. I just don't know if I could ever survive that again. I need to know that I can trust you with my heart." He is already nodding at me.

"You can trust me."

"I didn't just lose Evan. I almost lost Rachel. I didn't really care about the friends I lost, but I hated that they all knew about it before me. I don't want to live through that again. I need to know that you'll always be honest with me. No secrets. I can't be in a relationship with someone who would be ok with keeping me in the dark." I look into his eyes and watch as something passes through them. He blinks a few times and the pause he's taking makes my stomach drop with worry. Does he know something else?

"You have to trust me that I'll only ever do what's best for you above anyone else. You put your trust into a kid that never put you first. I'm asking you to put your trust in a man that would never be happy unless you were." With his words, the last little wall that I had worked so hard to build up around my heart crumbles and I can almost feel the sensation of floating as my heart falls completely for Andrew.

Chapter 16

Andrew

I sat across from her as she ate the breakfast I prepared for us and wondered if I was doing the right thing. She told me how important trust is to her and how badly Evans betrayal had hurt her and I held back the information about him cheating on Rachel until a few months ago. It might be a huge mistake that will come back to get me, but for right now I think it's best if she doesn't know.

Telling her about the cheating would put her in the middle. If she didn't tell Rachel and Rachel found out that she knew, it would surely end their friendship. It would eat away at Sophie keeping that secret from her best friend even if she never found out. If she told Rachel about it, it could have a huge effect on their marriage and Sophie would always be seen as the girl that helped to break them up. For now, I just have to know that I'm doing what's best for her and hope she will understand.

Listening to her talk about California was both exciting and heart breaking. She loves it there and plans to live there for a long time. Her face lights up each time she talks about her roommates and how wonderful it is to walk outside without being hit my that humid stale air we have here in Florida. At the same time, knowing that she is going to leave in two days to go back to her life there without me hurts. I feel like I finally got my chance to show her how much I've always cared about her and she's leaving.

We hung out at my place all morning and took a walk downtown to have lunch a few hours later. I held her hand and even stopped and kissed her a few times right on the street because I didn't want to waste a minute of the time we have together. I don't care who sees how much I love her, but know that keeping a low profile around the wedding guests is truly what's best for her. She's already had to put up with years of shame and constant rumors about what had happened between her and Evan. I won't pull her back into that spotlight with any of my actions.

At lunch, over a sandwich we shared, she told me about how hard it is at times to be away from her family. I understand that feeling well, both my parents left Florida for the much drier climate of Arizona to help with my father's allergies and arthritis. I try to visit them as often as possible, usually stopping in when I travel back and forth to California. I think leaving your friends and family just out of high school makes you a very courageous person and probably ages you quicker than your peers. I know each time that I look into her eyes that she is an old soul, wise beyond her years.

"Where are you boys going tonight?" she asks as I run my hand down her hair. Her finger is tracing circles on my bare chest as we lie in my bed. I love having her head on my chest and her body pressed closely to mine.

"A strip club. Nothing says cheesy bachelor party like greased up silicone, five inch heels and gold stripper poles." She laughs and I feel my own smile stretch across my face. I could listen to her laugh all day. It's like being back in grade school when I would do whatever it took to make a girl laugh. She brings out the playful kid in me. It's amazing just how much she brings out in me period. One minute I'm like a child, messing around and having the best time, and the next I'm all grown up thinking about white picket fences and two point five kids.

"Well, as long as one of them is named after some type of baking ingredient—Sugar, Chocolate, Cinnamon or something, I think your mission will be accomplished." This time I laugh, peeking down at her as she looks up at me.

"What about the girls? What are you doing?"

"Drinking and dancing," she rolls her eyes. "Can't say we achieved bachelorette party success unless everyone wakes up tomorrow with sore feet and regrets."

"I'm pretty good at massages. Keep that in mind when you're all liquored up and looking for a place to elevate your feet." I try hard to keep a straight face but fail when she pretends to be shocked. We both laugh and I pull her up higher on me so that I can kiss her lips. "I'm serious though, stay the night with me again. I'll give you my extra key."

"You just want me to help with all the left over excitement from the strip club. Maybe I'll wear my five inch heels."

"Strippers aren't really my thing. I'm sure the girls will be lovely, but I prefer the girl next door to lubed up tanning bed addicts. But, you should definitely wear the heels just incase."

My phone rings from the side table next to my bed. I pick it up and see that it's Evan. Sophie lies back down on my chest as I answer the call. "Hey Evan, what's up?"

"Where are you? We're going to leave a little early and grab a burger before the club." I can hear some of the guys in the background and feel a little bad for not being there with him.

"What time is it?" We haven't paid much attention to the time. After returning from lunch, we headed straight for my bed and haven't been out of it since. I don't keep a clock in here.

"Almost five."

"Shit. Sorry. I ran home to do a few things before the club. I'll head back now. Just text me where you'll be and I'll catch up. I can drop my car back off after dinner." Sophie sits up, pulling the sheet with her as she gets out of bed. I watch her go, hating that I can't just stay here with her tonight. She smiles at me over her shoulder as she makes her way into my bathroom.

"No problem. I'll text you when we're on our way. You might even make it back to the hotel before some of these douche bags are ready to go." I hear the sound of the phone moving across his chin as he purposefully yells, "They take longer than the fucking girls. Hurry up and finish putting on your make-up, some of us are hungry." I chuckle when I hear the curses and insults being flung his way from some of our friends.

"Thanks. I'll see you in a bit." I hang the phone up and make my way into the bathroom. I might not have all night here with her, but I do have at least another twenty minutes before the guys get their shit together and head out.

I drop Sophie off at the front of the hotel. I don't want to run the risk of anyone being in the lobby when if I walk her to her room. She promises to text me when she's on her way back up to my room tonight and I give her one last kiss. I text Evan and he lets me know that they just ordered their first round and burgers. His net text is the name of the burger joint. It isn't my favorite, but at least I know where it is. Sometimes my partners and I stop there after court to grab something to eat before heading home.

As I drive the short distance, I can't stop smiling. It finally feels like everything is falling into place. I'm the happiest I've ever been and I know it has everything to do with Sophie being back in my life. I'm a twenty-two year-old man who is hoping the night at the strip club will go by quickly so that I can rush back to be with her. I shake my head and laugh as I pull into the parking lot.

Once inside, I push the thoughts of her out of my mind and tell myself to focus on Evan. We order another round of drinks and I open a tab for all of the guys. We eat our burgers and a few of the guys flirt with the waitresses. Evan of course flirts too, but I decide to cut him some slack since this is technically his last nigh of being unmarried. My phone vibrates in my pocket and I slide my finger across the screen, pulling up a message from Sophie.

Sophie: Do these heels match my dress?

My heart races and I feel heat rush throughout my body. Attached to the message is a picture of her in a skin tight dress, so short I know there is no way she has any plans of bending even a little. Her breasts are pushed together giving me a perfect view of smooth cleavage. She's wearing a delicate necklace that rests on the curves of her breasts. It takes me a minute to even notice the heels, but as soon as I do I feel my lips curl up into a grin.

She has on the highest pair of heels I've ever seen. They might even put stripper heels to shame. Her long toned legs rise out of the bright heels and seem to travel for miles before any fabric makes an attempt at covering the apex of her thighs. She's so unbelievably hot I'm having trouble closing the image on my phone.

Me: I have no idea if they match, sweetheart, but I can tell you that they're perfect. Maybe I'll have you keep them on.

I send the text and then tuck my phone back into my pocket. If she sends me any more pictures tonight I'm going to have to cut the evening short and crash the girl's party instead. I look up to see Evan's eyes on me and an angry scowl on his face. I don't look away, deciding that it's time he realizes he lost his chance.

"I can't believe you man," he says when the guys leave us alone at the table to try to firm up plans to meet up with a few of the girls after work. "I thought we were friends. Now you're swooping in to take my sloppy seconds."

"There's nothing sloppy about it Evan. Get your head out of your ass and realize it's been four years. I've waited long enough." I tip the beer bottle to my lips and keep my eyes on him as I drink.

"Whatever. You'll get bored like I did after a while. She's the marrying kind, not the fun to fuck kind. Don't burn that little black book just yet." I know he's already drunk from pre-gaming in his room and the few rounds we've had here, but hearing him say those words has me wanting to rip him off his chair and beat the shit out of him.

"Maybe you just didn't know how girls worked back then. Don't worry about me my friend, I know what I'm doing." With my words his face turns red. I finish my beer and place the empty bottle back on the table. "We've been friends for along time now Evan. I didn't let her get between us in high school, so don't put her there now. That was the last time I'm going to sit back and let you put her down. Next time we are going to go outside and handle it like men. I'll leave our friendship at the door and beat the shit out of you."

The muscles of his jaw twitch as he clamps his teeth down but doesn't say anything. He sets his beer bottle down next to mine and pushes away from the table. I watch him stalk over to the guys who are chatting up the two female bartenders. I know as I watch him lean in closer to the woman behind the bar that our friendship is not going to recover from this. I'll do my duty tomorrow as his best man, and then I'll step away from this friendship because there hasn't been a benefit in it for me in years. Sometimes it's just time to realize that it's possible to out grow your best friend.

Chapter 17

S ophie

Standing in front of the long mirror of the hotel room closet, I spin around one last time and bend over to get a good idea of just how much room I have to move before I'm flashing anyone. This trip has gone so differently than I planned and as crazy as it sounds, I'm actually looking forward to spending the night celebrating with Rachel. It helps that this is a girls only night so I know that Evan won't be making an appearance.

My phone chimes with a message from Andrew and my stomach flips a million times in the split second it takes me to pull it up on the screen. I've never sent a man a picture or a text that alluded to anything sexual, but he brings out that playful side of me. I also trust him, which is huge for me.

Andrew: Have fun tonight, sweetheart. I'll see you later. Don't keep me waiting too long.

I don't get a chance to respond before there's a knock at my door. I open it up and Rachel squeals before pulling me into her arms. She smells like cinnamon whiskey and bad decisions. "SOPHIE!! I'm getting married tomorrow!" Her words slur together and I grab her elbow when she releases me from the hug and stumbles back a little. I shoot the other girls a judgmental stare for letting her get this messed up before the night has even began.

We take a car service to a club not too far from our hotel. Being out of state gave me the perfect excuse to not be the go-to person for planning this night. Her second in charge, Kristin, set the night up. She gives Rachel a piece of paper with what looks like a BINGO board on it and announces to us that she must complete the tasks on the board and we have to help her. I glance over Rachel's shoulder and read along with her as she reads them aloud.

"Give a hot guy a spank. Flash a guy. Give a stranger a lap dance," she giggles as the list goes on and I cringe knowing that this night is not only going to be filled with drunk girls and tacky pink furry tiaras, it will also include public humiliation and lots of evidence that single girls should not be in charge of the bride BINGO board. "Oooo, look! Let a man take a shot from between your boobs!" Great.

I slink down in my seat with a fake smile plastered on my lips and pull my phone out from my clutch even though I swore to myself I would not be the girl on the phone the whole night. Change of plans.

Me: Looks like we're playing whore BINGO.

Andrew: Wow. I'll try anything once.

Me: Haha. Not me and you. The girls! Too bad I left my flashing neon SLUTS sign for above our heads at home.

Andrew: While you would need the sign, trust me when I say your company doesn't. Men can see those girls coming from a mile away.

Rachel is still reading the list as Kristin begins to pass around a bright pink flask. This night is getting out of hand real fast.

Andrew: I've got to go. We are about to welcome Honey to the stage.

I laugh when I read his text and a few of the girls look in my direction. "Funny Facebook meme," I say and the flask is thrust in my direction. I take a long swig just to fit in and then put my arm around Rachel and lean back in to read the remaining items on the list. All are equally cringe worthy.

Once inside, it doesn't take long for Rachel to start working her way through the list. I sit back and watch, praying that none of her friends whip out their cell phones and document any of this. Not that Evan should be kept in the dark, but I guess anything that happens tonight will probably not go over too well in the morning. So far all of the men have played along, not that I would expect anything different since they're all getting to look at, rub or actually lick some part of her anatomy.

Finally when she has accomplished her BINGO we take to the dance floor. As I dance with Rachel I let myself remember the good times that we've had over the years. We were on Cheer together and before that we would spend our time dancing in my room or putting on shows for our parents. I realize that every fond memory I have of her is back when our relationship was still innocent. It was before we ever saw each other as competition or worried if people liked us enough.

Out of the corner of my eye I see a man approaching Rachel with a drink. When he finally makes his way to us, he leans into the group and practically yells, "I bought your friend a drink." She reaches for it, but I pull her hand away. Some of the girls look annoyed with me, but I don't care.

"No thanks. We've got her covered." I pull her a little closer to me and put myself between her and the drink. Who knows what could be in it?

"Come on. Don't be a party pooper." He moves a little closer, holding his arm out further this time so that Rachel can grab it. I look at her, and shake my head. She knows better than this. I think maybe she is just too wrapped up in the excitement of a man giving her attention.

"Sounding a little desperate, buddy." I say to him as I stop dancing.

Finally Rachel speaks up, "She's right. Thanks, but I'm only drinking what they're buying. She shrugs her shoulders and then smiles at me before starting to dance again. It's in this moment that I realize getting drunk is not an option for me tonight. If I'm going to be the only one looking out for her then I need to be sober. The thought of getting through this without alcohol isn't as daunting as it was when I saw it in the email a few weeks ago. It's amazing how one person can change your whole outlook on something.

My feet are aching by the time Kristin pulls us off the dance floor an hour later. She ushers us over to a private seating area in the back of the club that is decorated with bright pink streamers and feathers. It's like the Jersey Shore puked all over our area. Leopard print meets hot pink everywhere. We all squeeze into the booth and I take the seat next to Rachel, finally relaxing and enjoying this time with her.

Kristin digs through her large tote bag while we place our orders with the cocktail waitress. My order of ice water goes unnoticed by the other girls and I listen as they talk about boyfriends and school. I wonder if I would be more like them if I had stayed. I'm not sure anymore if I was a different person before I left, or if getting away from here is what changed me. Too many things were going on in my life at the time to be able to say for sure.

Finally Kristin's hand emerges with a notebook and a stack of papers. She perches herself at the edge of the table so that everyone can hear her. "Ok, ladies! It's time for the next game." I feel like rolling my eyes but hold back. I wish that we could just all hang out together and dance. I'm not a big fan of games. She puts the notebook down and hands us each a piece of paper with ten questions on it. Reaching back into her tote, she pulls out a box of pens and tosses it onto the center of the table.

The questions are all about Rachel. She is sitting back, sipping on her drink as we try to answer each of them. The first few are easy for me: her birthdate, parent's names and favorite color. I wonder is she remembers my favorite color. Next it asks her college major, her dream job, and favorite place to shop. I write down my answers, but the questions are beginning to make me realize that she and I don't share as much as we used to.

I remember talking about our college applications and her dreams of becoming a nurse. I also remember shopping with her at Nordstrom's or a small little boutique by the beach. But that was years ago. In the past four years our conversations have been more surface level. I hear her gripes about classmates or how annoying her roommates in the dorms are, but we haven't had a heart-to-heart in forever.

I take a minute to look around the table at all of the women frantically filling out the questionnaire, laughing at shared memories. I miss my friend more in this moment than I have in the last four years. It's just so blaringly obvious we've let our friendship slip. I feel guilty for holding her relationship with Evan against her. The last four questions I can't even answer. I don't know her new address, have no idea how many children she wants to have, where she bought her dress, or what song she and Evan will dance to for the first time as husband and wife.

Setting my pen down on the table, I wait as the other woman squeal and giggle. Kristin asks us to hand them in and then she gives the stack to Rachel to decide the winner. She laughs at a few of the answers and shuffles the papers before looking over mine. I watch as her smile drops when she sees my answers for the last four questions. Instead of some elaborate guess, I answered them as honestly as possible.

7. Sorry.

8. I

9. Miss

10. You

Her eyes fill with tears and she pushes the stack of papers away from herself and pulls me in for a tight hug. "I miss you, too," she says in a whisper. The girls at the table have no idea what I wrote and I imagine they think this is some great moment where I answered everything about her perfectly. This week I'm getting to a place where I might be able to honestly say that I forgive her for not waiting longer or considering my feelings before dating my ex. I'm not saying I'll ever forget it; just feeling like enough time has passed to stop picking the scab off the wound.

She wipes her eyes and laughs as she picks up the stack of papers. "Just give the prize to Gina, I think she could use it." Gina claps her hands and then holds them out to Kristin awaiting her prize. A tube of edible chocolate body butter is placed in them and her cheeks turn pink under all the stares. It's adorable and appropriate so I laugh along with the rest of them.

After the waitress returns with another round, Kristin is back to her perch at the edge of the table. This time she says something to the waitress we can't hear, and then starts flipping through the notebook. The waitress returns with a row of shot glasses. Six clear shot glasses of vodka are lined up in front of Rachel and her eyes grow big.

"Does everyone have a drink of their own?" Kristin shouts at us and we each raise our drinks for her to see. "For this game I'm going to ask Rachel a question that I had Evan answer. If she gets it right, we all have to take a big sip of our drinks. No cheating—go big. If she gets it wrong, she has to take the shot." We all hoot and holler as Rachel lifts a shot glass in Kristin's direction.

"I've totally got this. Fire away." She's already drunk so I'm hoping that she knows most of the answers so we don't have to carry her out of here.

"What sports did Evan play in High School?" I think to myself, football and cross country as soon as Kristin completes the sentence.

"Um, running…no, cross country and football." Rachel smiles at us confidently.

"That's right, ladies. Drink up!" We all take a drink and let out a small cheer when we're done. Kristin waits until we put our drinks back down. "What was his football number?" Again, the answer, twenty-four, flashes in my head.

"Rachel thinks for a minute and then answers, "Twenty-seven?" Kristin shakes her head and points to the shot glass. Rachel shrugs a shoulder and downs the liquid, earning her a cheer when it doesn't come right back up.

"Where was his favorite place to eat in high school?"

Rachel throws her head back laughing, "Beer and Burgers."

"That's right." We all take another drink and I begin to grow uncomfortable with this game. "What was his order?" Cheeseburger, no onions, extra sauce and ranch for his fries. I look right at Rachel as she hesitates. Kristin thinks this game is fun, but she has no idea how awkward this whole thing is. I was the one who dated him in high school, not Rachel. He broke up with me the last week of June in 2010, a week after our graduation.

"I don't remember. It was a long time ago." She answers with a little laugh but I can tell she's growing anxious.

Kristin doesn't let her off the hook. "He told me a cheese-burger, no onions, extra sauce and a side of ranch for his fries. Drink up buttercup!" Rachel salutes us with the shot glass before downing it. "What is Evan's favorite holiday?" The Fourth of July. I hate that I know all of these things about him. Why won't my brain just stay out of this stupid game?

This time when Rachel looks at me there's no humor on her face. I mouth the answer to her, but she just keeps her eyes on me and lifts her glass in the air. A little bit of the vodka sloshes out and I know she is definitely feeling the alcohol.

"I don't know this one either." She finally turns her head back to Kristin and downs the glass. She laughs as she sets the glass down and I take a second to glance around at the other women. They have no idea what's happening, it's like they're on a completely wavelength than Rachel and I. Of course, Rachel is acting like none of it matters. She's the queen of playing things off.

"Before wanting to be an accountant, what did Evan want to be growing up?" Kristin hasn't even finished before Rachel's eyes are burning into mine. This time I don't try to mouth the answer, policeman, to her. I just stare back. She knows I can answer it and the reality that I might know him better is now blatantly obvious to the both of us.

She puts her fingers on the rim of her vodka shot but keeps her eyes on me. This feels horrible. She's hurting and I can't do anything about it. I give her my best comforting face, but she just shakes her head and sucks down the vodka without any laughing or smiles. This time the table gets quiet. All eyes are on us and it feels like an old western duel. I won't pull my weapon and she should know that. I would never embarrass her in front of people. It doesn't even matter if I know the answers anyway, he chose her.

Kristin quickly flips the page in her notebook and I'm hoping she has finally figured out that she needs to ask a question only Rachel and Evan will know the answer to. Something AFTER me. "Where did you and Evan have sex for the first time together." I breathe a sign of relief and close my eyes for just a second, feeling my heart slow down.

"In the backset of his truck." This time she smiles and I know that she has to be right. I feel the tension between us fade as she looks up to a confused Kristin.

"No, he said in your room," Kristin corrects looking back at the paper like his answer might magically change right before her eyes. At this point, the whole table is looking back and forth from Rachel to Kristin, much like the audience at a tennis tournament. I feel a wave of unease rush over me as I look at my best friend. She's already shaking her head, her eyes hazy from the alcohol. She leans forward, resting her elbows on the table, knocking over one of the empty shot glasses. The awkward tension at the table reaches a fever pitch.

"I told you, it was in the backseat of his truck. I remember it because he was all sweaty from the football game and the windows started fogging up." Her words are slurring and she starts to giggle with the memory. "I can't believe he could forget that," she reaches for her shot glass in another sloppy move that has the entire table watching her closely. I think maybe it's time to call it a night and take her back to the hotel.

Kristin shrugs her shoulder and says, "I didn't realize he played football in college."

"He didn't. It was our senior year after the last game." Her words fade out as if she realizes what she's saying, but can't stop them. Her eyes flash up to mine and she covers her mouth as a collective gasp is heard from the other women. A quick look around the table confirms what I already know. Not one of the women sitting here can look me in the eyes because they all knew it was happening and hadn't told me. I feel my heart break in my chest. It's the worst pain that I've ever felt, worse than the day Evan broke up with me or the day she told me they were dating. Hearing her accidently admit to having sex with my boyfriend six months before he and I broke up nearly kills me.

She reaches out quickly for my wrist, but I pull it away and push myself back from her. "Don't!" I manage as I feel the bile rising in my throat. I'm going to be sick.

"Please, Sophie. I'm sorry. I'm so sorry," she cries, but I put my hands up to stop her.

"I need to get out of here. You need to move." I look her straight in the eye, my voice stern and unwavering.

"No, I won't. We need to fix this."

"Get out of the fucking booth Rachel!" I feel my last bit of restraint snap and then it's gone. All that's left is the unrelenting burning rage that her betrayal has ignited within me.

unrelenting burning rage that her betrayal has ignited within me.

Chapter 18

Andrew

The stripper slides her greased up body around the pole and makes eye contact with Evan. She knows exactly who to butter up to get the best tips. He was drunk a few hours ago and now it's just getting old to watch him toss money onto the stage in a very demeaning manner. A few of the other guys have joined me in a booth towards the back of the club and we're sipping on our drinks waiting anxiously for Evan to tell us he's done for the night or pass out.

I pull my phone out of my pocket and check for new messages from Sophie. I haven't heard from her in over two hours and I'm starting to wonder if she drank a little too much and is going to cancel our plans to meet up tonight. I shouldn't feel as disappointed as I do, but that doesn't seem to matter as I tap the fingers of my free hand on the table and pray that this night is almost over. She never answered my last text and I'm trying hard not to be that needy guy who sits around waiting on texts from a girl he isn't even in a relationship with.

Finally, as the waitress brings another round to the table with an empathetic smile, I decide I lost the battle and pull my phone from my pocket for the sole purpose of connecting with Sophie.

Andrew: Hey sweetheart. Everything ok?

I watch the screen for the small dotted bubble that would let me know she is typing a message back, but instead my phone screen dims and then goes dark all together. I toss it onto the table in front of me and run my hand down my face and over the stubble of my chin.

A few more of the guys wander back to our table and scoot into the booth, watching Evan continue to make an ass out of himself. Soon he's alone, sitting back in his chair nursing his whiskey. I figure he's probably going to be out of cash soon and we can get out of this place before the light of the morning creeps through the dark blinds shaming all of us for having wasted this entire evening in such a shady place.

Andrew: I think we are going to leave soon. How about you?

Once again there is no sign of her and I feel my heart pick up its pace and my stomach knot with the helpless feeling of being stuck here instead of finding Sophie and making sure she made it home safe. What if she drank too much? Would anyone be looking out for her? I let my head fall back against the booth and close my eyes, fighting off the frustration and growing need to beat the shit out of my friend. I'm clearly not the only one; a few other guys keep checking their phones either for the time or texts from late night booty calls.

The bartender shouts, "Last call!" and I sit up straight, suddenly feeling excited again. We make our way over to Evan and pull him from the chair. I have no idea how he's going to get up and look anywhere near presentable for his wedding tomorrow, but I don't give a shit. I want to get out of here and find Sophie. We push through the doors of the club and climb into a few taxi vans, heading back to the hotel. My phone is running out of battery, no doubt from all the times I've unlocked the screen hoping to have missed a text from her.

Andrew: On our way back. Where are you?

This time my text shows that she saw it and I feel a small window of relief until ten minutes pass and she doesn't respond. Now I'm starting to freak out. What the hell? Maybe she found a guy at the bar? Maybe she passed out in her room? All the possibilities are making me feel nauseous. I hate not knowing if she's ok and my curiosity is putting me on edge.

As soon as we step out of the taxi, I bring up her name in my contacts and click send. The phone rings in my ear just once before her voicemail connects. Did she just deny my call? Maybe she's just in a bad patch for cell service. I call again and immediately her voice mail picks up. Now I'm in a full panic. The guys are making their way to the front doors of the hotel and I run a few steps to catch up with them.

My plan is to find Rachel and ask where she is, but as the doors slide open I can see that the bride-to-be is sobbing in the lobby, sinking down on a chair and getting lost in a pile of tissue. This is not good. "Where's Sophie?" I practically yell, startling all of the girls. A few of them look down to the ground while one forms a small "O" with her mouth. She's my new target. I know she can sense my intensity as I stare her down. "Where the hell is she?"

Rachel sobs and blows her nose noisily into a tissue as Evan finally realizes his fiancé is upset. He bends down and gives her an irritated look. "What's the matter now, Rachel? Florist doesn't have the perfect shade of orange?" His words are slurred and he stands back up to wave his arms around. "Can't be apricot, sherbert, monarch, goldfish, carrot, pumpkin or tangerine. NOOOO it has to be fucking burnt orange." He says the last name in a high-pitched girl voice that would have had me laughing if I wasn't so fucking worried about what happened to Sophie.

I flick my eyes back to the woman who is trying to comfort Rachel. "Where is she?"

"Well, um, she got a little upset tonight." She waves her hand as if it's nothing, but I take a step closer and her eyes go wide. "She took off about two hours ago. I haven't been able to get Rachel to calm down. She wanted to wait for

Evan."   From behind me I hear Evan let out an exasperated breath, "What the fuck am I supposed to do? She's always crying about something." His eyes meet his future bride's, "You need to get your shit together. You're a grown woman making a fucking scene in the lobby of a hotel that's filled with your guests!" He spins around and waves his arms to show her the lobby.

"She knows," Rachel wails and the girls around her suddenly seem very interested in the tile floor.

"What does she know?" I ask, unable to put all the pieces together in this fucked up aftermath of their last night before marriage. I feel like slamming my fist through something. If I don't get answers soon I'm going to lose my shit.

The girl draped over the edge of the large chair Rachel is slouched in finally makes eye contact with me. "She knows that Evan was having sex with Rachel while they were still together. It sort of just slipped out during one of the games." I see red immediately. The lobby around me becomes blurry at the edges as a rage so fierce it could shatter the walls flashes through me. I turn to look at my best friend who only shrugs a shoulder like it doesn't make him the biggest asshole in the world to have slept with his girlfriend's best friend while they were still dating.

It's like an out of body experience. It seems like I'm watching a movie play out in front of me instead of the reality taking place in the lobby of a fancy hotel. "You fucking cheated on her? Are you serious?" I want him to tell me it's a misunderstanding, but as far as miracles go, I'm pretty sure God is too busy with real issues to grant me this small favor. I shove Evan back so hard he falls, his ass sliding along the shiny slick surface of the lobby tile.

"It was a long time ago!" Evan answers, trying hard to right himself and brush off his jeans. "I'm not the one that spilled the beans. You want to blame someone, blame my chatty fiancé over there." He points to Rachel but I don't let my eyes stray from his for one second.

"You're such a selfish prick! Why the fuck would you sleep with Rachel when you had Sophie?" This leads to another wail from the soggy bride-to-be. "Are you that fucking stupid? You're a liar! How could you let her come here when you've done such a horrible thing to her?" My shouting has alerted the hotel staff of an impending fight and I watch as security begins to make their way over to us.

"You know me," Evan says with another shrug, "I'm not gonna turn down a girl that's throwing it at me. Sophie was hot, but totally inexperienced. You can't be pissed that I looked for it other places. I'm a guy. That's what we do." Now Rachel screams and lunges from the chair, but I beat her to him. My fist slams into his face, fueled by hate and vehemence.

One after another I rain down my knuckles into the reddened skin of his face, feeling the give of bone beneath my fists. It's been a long time coming so if security wants to save this asshole's life they better move a little quicker. As if this wasn't already the most shameful display of adult behavior that has ever taken place in the lobby of this five star hotel, I hear a battle cry from Rachel as she lurches towards us, a trail of used tissues littering her path. I brace for her impact, but she passes me and dishes out her own punishment to Evans face. When the security guard pulls me off of him, she moves right in trying hard to clamp her little hands around his neck and slam his unconscious head onto the tile below them.

Now cops begin to rush into the lobby and I'm pushed aside as they tackle Rachel and smash her face into the floor beside Evan. Her friends watch in horror as she resists arrest and is once again slammed into the hard floor with a sharp cry. I expect that the next person to enter this lobby might be Jerry Springer, but within minutes the whole thing is over and security is questioning everyone.

Evan comes to in the back of the ambulance just before they are about to take him in. He quickly refuses medical attention and gives me an apologetic look as he tries hard to tell the cops the whole thing was his fault. He explains that tomorrow is the wedding and if everyone gets arrested there would be a lot of disappointed people and a ton of money down the drain. The older cop who appears to be in charge gives him a warning and a few tickets, but ultimately releases all of us with the stern threat that he will be arresting everyone if he gets called back here.

I don't wait for the elevator. I take the stairs two at a time until I fling open the door that leads to her hallway.

Chapter 19

S ophie

I'd like to be able to say that once again I was the bigger person. If that were true, I would've forgiven Rachel and returned to my hotel room to sleep off the funk of finding out what a bitch she really is. Maybe I would have woken up refreshed and chipper, anxiously awaiting the day that I would get to see my best friend walk down the aisle to her future. Well, fuck that. This time I'm not the bigger person and it feels fantastic!

My aching heart still stings with the reminder of how I was fooled by both of them for quite some time, but I have a little peace in knowing it will never happen again. For the first time ever in my life, I have waged a war against an enemy and I don't plan on taking any prisoners. I'd like to say that I handled this like a lady, but if I'm honest, the first ten minutes of my biggest heartbreak was not very pretty.

I shoved Rachel out of the booth and after shouting a few choice words to her and all the backstabbing women who allowed me to remain in the dark, I threw a fit in the parking lot. I'm pretty sure I looked like a woman losing herself to madness as I screamed out loud and stomped my feet like a little kid. Then, the fog of my deception cleared and I got down to business.

As the plane takes off, I lean back in my seat with a contented smile on my lips, breathing out the vodka laced breath as passengers begin to fill the empty seats around me. A little giggle erupts from my chest as I think about how tomorrow will play out for my former bestie and her lying cheating asshole of a future husband. My seatmate looks down at me from where he's standing in the aisle, puzzled at how he's going to fit his carryon into the overhead.

I guess when you see a woman with a tear-streaked face, dressed like a streetwalker approach your station to board a plane you try to look the other way when she's carrying on something as ridiculous as a million pounds of wadded up tulle and chiffon. The flight attendant has now made her way over and she carefully assesses the situation.

"Miss, could I hang this up for you? Maybe it would give everyone a little more room to store their things." She looks at me sympathetically as she points to the torn ratted remains of Rachel's wedding dress. I smile up at her and nod my head.

"Thanks. That would be awesome." I don't move to help her yank the tattered dress from the compartment, but I do see the knowing look she exchanges with the man waiting to store his items. They think I've lost my mind. I however, think this is the most clear my head has been in years.

My phone buzzes again and I see Andrew's name flash across the screen. My heart clenches again and I feel the roll of nausea hit me as I shut down my phone for the flight. His little speech makes perfect sense now. He had told me that I would need to believe that he would know what is best for me. That I should trust him if he ever kept something from me, but I now know his secret and I think he's almost as horrible as they are for allowing me to attend the stupid week of celebration for the people who were screwing behind my back in high school.

As we begin our taxi down the runway, I stare out at the dark night just outside my small window. What a turn of events. The lights twinkle back at me as we gain speed and I close my eyes and lean back against the headrest. Her missing wedding dress will probably be her first discovery and I almost wish I could see her face when she frantically tries to find it. Hopefully my burnt orange bride's maid dress will be an ok substitute.

She'd given me her key to the room so that I could make sure she was tucked into bed safely at the end of the night. I decided that perhaps she should be taught a little lesson in trust; after all I had trusted her and she had showed me what a big mistake that was. I also helped myself to her wedding binder, you know that ridiculously large planner that contained every tiny detail of tomorrow. Thank you, Rachel, for making this so easy.

I'm sure there are many wedding vendors that are used to last minute changes. They all seemed so nice to answer my very late night/early morning calls. With a steady voice, I happily informed them of a few changes I would like to make to my wedding plans. You see, it's hard to argue with a bride who can tell you exactly where to switch something out for another.

For instance, when I told the DJ that my future husband and I had made a last minute decision to go with a song that held some sentiment, he got a little excited. I guess always playing the same boring songs for first dances can really wear on a man. He was happy to substitute Patty Loveless' Blame it on Your Heart for the first dance in place of the cheesy Elvis song when I explained to him that it was the first song we ever danced to as a couple. I assured him all of our guests knew the history behind it, but it might be helpful remind everyone that the song represented a special time in our relationship.

The wedding cake baker was a little harder to convince when I told her that I had been thinking about how left out my close friends would feel if they too were not represented on the top of our cake. She tried hard to reason with me that it's really only traditional to have a bride and groom as cake toppers, but I insisted she put a few more female figures up on top of the cake. With an exhausted sign she reluctantly agreed to add my requested entourage. It's only right that I adjust the cake plans to more accurately depict the relationship it's helping to christen.

The last of the vendors was very excited about the last minute change. I agreed that it was very charitable for Rachel and Evan make a donation to a cause in the name of each guest instead of giving out cheap wedding favors. How very big of them. I'm just happy that the coordinator was as big of an advocate for safe sex as I am. I worried it might be a tough sell to change the chosen charity from the very ineffective one that Rachel had chosen just to look good to one that offers free STD screening and pregnancy tests to the community. The very appreciative woman on the line assured me that all the cards placed at each seat would proudly display the new charity and their mission.

With my evil plan in full swing, and Rachel's wedding binder on it's way down to the very bottom of the first swampy river I found, I'm able to relax again. My roommates are waiting for my plane to arrive and have promised to have a freezer stocked full of the necessary ice cream to get me through the heartache I know is going to hit me as soon as the adrenaline wears off. In the mean time, I'm going to try to get some sleep so this departure from hell won't seem to take as long.

Just as I begin to drift off to sleep, I smile with the memory of calling my mother to warn her of my absence tomorrow. I'd worried she would freak out about my plan, but upon hearing the detail of Evan and Rachel's disgusting secret, she offered to stand guard at Rachel's door as I began phase one of burning the already dilapidated bridge of our friendship. My father didn't weigh in, just nodded his head when I emerged from the room with shreds of the dress dragging along the ground behind me.

I don't think that my actions will affect their marriage, maybe the ceremony a touch but not the actual vows they will say to each other. As much as I wish it were different, I have learned that a person is who they are and I can't change that. If Rachel wants to be a liar and insists on competing with me, then I have no way of influencing her choices. If Evan is going to be a selfish asshole that constantly cheats on the women he's with, then there isn't anything I could do about that either. The only part of this whole mess that seems so unjust is that I can't do anything to make Andrew change his natural inclination to protect his best friend at all costs. In the end, he chose his best friend over my heart.

Chapter 20

Andrew

How are there no flights out of this town until tomorrow? I sit on the edge of my bed and rest my head in my hands. It looks like Sophie caught the last plane out of here and now all I can do is wait around until the flights resume tomorrow. My bags are packed and my ticket is purchased. This time if she is fleeing this town, I'm going with her. I will not make the same mistake I did four years ago when I let her board a plane and fly out of my life.

Maybe this is not the best thought out plan, but I can't take a chance that she is going to try to push me out of her life with out even letting me explain. I had no idea that Evan cheated on her with Rachel. My secret I was keeping from her was that he had been cheating on Rachel. I didn't think it was in her best interest to know that if she had to stand up there with Rachel. I guess now that I was very wrong. Asking her to trust me only lead her to believe that I knew about Evan and Rachel.

I pace my room watching the numbers on the clock slowly change, mocking my need to get face-to-face with her so she can see in my eyes that I'm not lying. I would have never allowed her to go through with this week if I had known earlier. Evan was my best friend, but I'm not a heartless dick like he is. What he and Rachel did to Sophie is unforgivable and I would have never kept that from her.

Evan's texts start blowing up my phone an hour before I'm about to leave for the airport. He is apologizing for our fight and asking me to help him fix things with Rachel. I don't answer any of them. I also don't answer the door when he knocks on it ten minutes later. My exit from his life is going to be swift. There's no need to drag out this dying friendship any longer.

The taxi pulls to the edge of the parking lot and I climb inside. The worker that's changing the marque in front of the hotel waves as we drive by. So far the new message proudly says, "Congratulations Evan and Rachel." As we wait for the light to change, he adds, "On your pregnancy." I feel my brows furrow together and then the realization hits me that Sophie might have something to do with the hilarious new message. Good for her.

As we make our way through the traffic of the now busy airport, I begin to receive a second wave of frantic texts from Evan and then eventually Rachel. Evan is freaking out because apparently his face is swollen and no amount of ice is making it better. Also, apparently his grandparents would like to know why they were not told about the baby and will not believe that Evan has no idea what they're talking about.

Rachel's texts are a little more insistent. She wants to know if I have seen Sophie. She would also like to know if I've seen her wedding gown. I don't feel sorry for her for even a second after what she did and I hope that if Sophie had anything to do with all the strange things happening today, she's going to one day be able to see all the chaos beautifully documented on Facebook.

My thoughts have not left her all night and all morning. I pray that I didn't destroy what we were building and that she'll allow me to do what ever it takes to make this better. It just doesn't seem fair that after all of these years of loving her from afar, I only got a few days with her and one unfor- gettable night. My stomach knots and I feel the ache in my heart grow as the time away from her ticks by.

Having her leave has shifted my world. I felt the loss of her from my life again and I know that it's not something I'm willing to live with. I've put a call into my assistant, Anna, at the office and let her know I will be in California for a while and to set up a meeting with the partners on Monday. I should know by then if Sophie will have me, and if she says yes, then I'm not going to ever let distance separate us again. I'm going to offer to head up the firm in California like they have been grooming me for this last year.

I should probably have a plan for if she tells me to leave, but thinking about that road only causes a panic to race through me and I just can't face that possibility right now. I move through the security line with only my small carryon and check my phone one last time before shutting it down. The picture that Evan just sent me of his swollen face is very amusing, but I still move my fingers quickly, blocking his future calls and texts.

As I step onto the plane, I over hear a few of the flight attendants talking about a woman who had left her wedding dress on the plane last night. They had tried to run after her, but she only smiled and told them to keep it. Word travels fast through the attendants apparently and I feel a small smile curve my lips as I picture a strong Sophie taking with her Rachel's most important accessory for today. I had never figured her for a vengeful woman, but I'm starting to love that about her. Knowing she didn't just roll over and take it any longer makes me very proud of her.

As the plane takes off, I realize that there's no other way this story could possibly end. Sophie and I are meant to be together and if it takes me the rest of my life to prove that to her, then let today be the first day of the rest of our lives. I reach down, pressing my hand to my pocket to make sure I remembered the keys to my condo in LA. While the plane closes the distance between Sophie and I, Anna is working hard to find her address for me. I guess it helps to have a few friends in the right places.

I grow increasingly more impatient as I wait for the people ahead of me to leave the plane. I feel like I'm losing ground the longer it takes to get to her. She could have convinced herself by now that I'm as big of an ass as Evan. Maybe her friends are even telling her to stay away from me. I wouldn't blame them one bit. Finally I emerge from the plane and quickly make my way to baggage claim, firing up my phone to talk to Anna.

"Anna, did you get it?" I sound desperate and that's because I am. She laughs softly into the phone as I hold my breath waiting for her answer.

"You owe me big for doing this on my day off. I talked to your friend at the station. He came up with the address from her driver's license. Of course I had to promise him we would never say where we got the info from, but he was happy to pay back the favor he owed you for getting him out of that legal mess a year ago." I can hear a paper crinkling as she pauses to give me the information.

"Thanks Anna. I owe you. Can you text me the address?"

"Of course." I'm about to hang up when she says, "Oh, hey Andrew?"

"Yes?"

"This girl must be pretty special." It's a statement, but I can still hear the underlying question within the words.

"Yes, I think I've loved her since the day I first saw her. Now I just have to convince her to give me a shot." I feel my heart beat rapidly in my chest as I watch the bags begin to make their first circle around the track.

"I have my fingers crossed for you. Let me know how it goes." I thank her and we hang up as my bag finally makes its way to me. My phone chimes with Sophie's address, and I pull the bag from the belt and make my way out into the crisp Californian air. Jumping into the back of a taxi, I rattle off her address and hope that he gets there quickly.

We pull onto her street and I practically rip the handle off the door when the taxi stops right in front of her cute little apartment building. I pull my bag from the trunk and sling my carryon over my shoulder. I probably should ask the driver to wait here for me, but then that would require me admitting to myself that she might not want to hear what I have to say. Instead I ask for his card and hand him a wad of cash, eager to make my way up to her door.

Of course she is on the second floor and there is no elevator in sight in the old building. I'm a little out of breath by the time I make it to her doorstep, but then again that might be more from my speeding pulse and anxiety about seeing her than luging my bags up the stairs. I take a minute to calm down and then lift my hand and knock on her door. I find it ironic that I'm supposed to be standing at the end of an aisle with my best friend on the most important day of his life, and instead I am standing alone in front of a door that might just make this the best day of mine instead. Please, Sophie. Give us one more chance.

Chapter 21

S ophie

I'm halfway through my second pint of ice cream when there is a knock at the front door. Reluctantly I set down my pint and make my way over. My roommates sat up with me until the wee hours of the morning, but I finally released them from their duty and allowed them to leave me so they could join the land of the living. I had no plans to do that today, still having another of my favorite flavors waiting its turn in the freezer.

It didn't take long for my roommates to make me realize that I'd fallen for Andrew. With all the anger and disappointment I'd felt putting the pieces together that he had known about the two of them and not told me, I'd taken very little time to realize that my heart still wanted to be with him. I'm starting to think that Florida should be permanently removed from my travel itinerary as I'm always leaving my heart there when I return to California.

It had felt good to finally move on from Evan and open my heart up to love again, but now I'm stashed away in my dark apartment feeling right back where I started a week ago. Only now, my heart hurts all over again. Getting over Evan had been rough. He was my first and only love so I had no idea how to crawl out of the hole he left me in. Getting over Andrew is going to be just as painful, but for a different reason. Where I'd loved Evan deeply because he was my first, I love Andrew because he is the other half to my soul. If he hadn't kept something so big from me, I'd have run to him the second I found out the truth for his comfort.

Maybe that's why I fell deeper in the whole of heartache than ever before. I had faith in Andrew and hope that I wasn't completely inept at relationships. I lost that faith and hope in one sentence from the mouth of the horrible monster I used to call my best friend. I swallow down the lump that's in my throat again, a little angry that the numbing cold of the ice cream isn't doing better keeping it at bay. Shaking my head and swiping another tear, I reach for the door knob and hope it isn't someone wanting to offer me salvation, because I just don't think I have a nice bone left in my body right now.

My hair is pulled up in a very messy bun, and not the kind that you do on purpose, more like the knotted mess that happens when you hop a redeye home and immediately fall onto your couch in a puddle of tears and melted chocolate ice cream. I had managed to wash my face about an hour ago, but my eyes are swollen and still feel like I've put a handful of sand in each one. My favorite heartbreak outfit has made a return appearance and I tug a little at the old t-shirt and yoga pants before pulling the door open.

I don't expect to see Andrew on my doorstep, so his image steals my breath. He looks as handsome as always, but his hair is disheveled and clearly has been abused by nervous hands and a few hours of flying. His chin has some stubble and I can see in his eyes that the night has not been easy on him. When he takes in my appearance, his lips fall into a pained expression and I immediately look away because I feel tears threaten to fall again.

Andrew's strong hand reaches out and he wipes a small smudge of ice cream from the corner of my mouth before I can move. Having him so close to me again is making it hard to think and I'm trying to figure out if I want to throw myself in his arms so he can comfort me, or claw his eyes out and push him down the flight of stairs. Don't judge. It's been a rough week and I'm now functioning solely on sugar.

"What are you doing here?" My voice clearly sounding as frustrated as I feel.

"Whatever it takes to make you forgive me." He pulls the bag from his shoulder and lets it fall at his feel. "I didn't know Sophie. I swear on everything. I didn't know." I feel the breath escape my lungs again and this time a strangled sob escapes as well. My hand covers my mouth just a second before his strong arms are around me.

I can smell his familiar scent again as he holds me tightly to his chest. At first I don't move, but as he presses a kiss to the top of my head, I relax and wrap my arms around him. Maybe I should doubt him, be a little more cautious believing what he says, but I saw the truth in his eyes. No one would fly across the country and show up on my doorstep when he was supposed to be the best man in his childhood friend's wedding as we speak. And maybe, if I'm honest, I need to believe him because the thought of moving on without him is almost too much to bear.

"You said I needed to trust you." If he wasn't talking about Evan and Rachel then why did I need to trust him? His hand brushes up and down my back and I want so badly to have his words be enough. For the first time in a very long time, my instinct is to trust him and I'm praying his answer will but my head at ease and in agreement with my heart.

"Evan has been cheating on Rachel. He told me before he met up with you on the beach. I know I should have told you, but I thought you had already been through so much. I didn't want you to have to hold that secret or to be the one responsible for the wedding not happening. I just couldn't do that to you." He lightly grips my arms and pulls me back so he can look into my eyes. "I wanted you to trust me to protect you and make decisions that won't put you in a position where you will get hurt. I had no idea they were sleeping together in high school."

His eyes are focused on mine and I can see his desperation for me to believe him expressed in them. I shake my head a little and take a small step back. "You were best friends. How could you not know?" I just can't reconcile that in my head. They did everything together. He takes a deep breath and then slides his hands down my arms.

"I could say the same about you and Rachel." I feel a sharp stab of pain in my heart, but he's making perfect sense. She was my best friend and Evan was my boyfriend. I should have known. "They didn't want to get caught Sophie. They were doing something unforgivable and while they are both the biggest idiots I've ever met, they were smart enough to know that they would lose you." He tugs me a little closer and when our faces are just a few inches from each other he smiles. It's both warm and innocent and I feel my heart leap in my chest with his words. "Take it from me, Sophie. No one can bear the thought of losing you once you've been in their life."

He rests his forehead against my own and then in a voice that seems to be seeking out my soul he says, "I let you walk out of my life once because you had never belonged to me, but this time it's different. This time I've had a taste of what we could be like together and it's unbelievable. You just don't let that kind of thing go. I'm here because you deserve a man that's willing to wait for you, fight for you and fly across the country for a chance to stand on your doorstep and ask you for another chance with your heart." His face pulls away so that he's looking into my eyes again.

I feel the warm tears streaking down my face. I swallow down the emotion that's making it impossible to answer him. I know already that I'm going to give him a chance, but when I don't answer he kisses me softly before saying, "And you don't let the best woman to ever come into your life get revenge on the two people who so greatly deserve it without you." His hand drops from my arm and I watch as he reaches into his pocket.

Right now if they went through with it, Rachel and Evan are getting married. They're standing in front of their family and friends vowing to be faithful and to love each other forever. I've never been so grateful to not be a part of something in my life. As I look up into Andrew's eyes I realize that they're doing that without us because we're a team, and being here on my doorstep is more important to Andrew than being at what might be the most important day in Evan's life.

I'm not expecting what happens next, so when a small grin curls his lips I feel my stomach twist as he pulls a small black box out of his pocket. When he opens it, I can see that it contains a large gold band. He pulls the ring from the slit and tosses it in the air between us. "This, sweetheart, is the final phase of wedding day revenge." I can't help the smile that spreads across my face with the recognition that he has in his possession Evan's wedding band. He rubs his chin as if deep in thought. "So what are you thinking? Off the overpass onto the 405 freeway? Maybe watch sink into the dark water off of the pier?"

I throw my arms around his neck and pull his lips to mine. His arms circle around my waist and I finally feel at peace when his body is pressed against mine. When I finally come up for air I whisper, "You stole his ring for me?" I hear him laugh as he tucks his head into my neck and kisses a trail down to my shoulder.

"I would do anything for you."

I take a minute to feel his lips on my skin before pulling away again to look into his eyes. I put my hands on the side of his face and kiss him tenderly. "All I need is for you to love me." My heart pounds in my chest in the moment between my words and his.

His smile melts my insides as he sneaks in one last kiss, "Sophie, I already do."

Epilogue

Sophie

    I can smell the salt in the air as the perfect breeze flows in through the window. Cassidy is focusing hard on getting the fragile orchids in the perfect position above the curls that are loosely gathered just above my right shoulder. I'd thought I'd lost the opportunity to have a best friend when I ended my friendship with Rachel. Meeting Andrew's sister and falling right into a new friendship was unexpected. I guess it would make sense that I'd feel a connection to her since the connection I have with her brother is so strong.

    She steps back and gives me one last look from my bare feet up to where the soft white silk dances around my knees before curving tightly past my waist and stops at the top of my breasts in a beautiful heart shape. My tan skin stands out against the bright fabric, courtesy of all the time we've been spending at the beach, which is just a short walk from the quaint home we found. Our yard is full of roses and climbing wisteria, but the best feature is the small path that leads to the beach not too far from our front door.

There was never a question that we would stay in California. We've been in our little piece of paradise for just over a year after trying out a few other locations in the city. Cassidy smiles at me and then pulls me into a hug. A small knock at the door let's me know it's time to go and I grab the bouquets from the small table and hand Cassidy, my maid of honor, her flowers. It just felt right to have her stand up there with us as we made our vows to each other.

She opens the door and steps out onto the sand, accepting the waiting arm of Andrew's closet's friend, Aiden, from work. The two of them are always together, working on cases and helping each other out while building the firm's office in California. I don't miss the way he looks at her as if she hung the moon, or the way she blushes when his whispers that she looks beautiful.

I didn't think I could get any happier than this, but then y father steps up to my side and extends his arm for me to take. He kisses my cheek and I try to keep the tears at bay as we round the corner from the small bridal suite and begin our walk down the sandy aisle. A small wedding on the beach is perfect for us. They only people here are close family and a few friends. In case you're wondering, Evan and Rachel did not make the quest list. Not that they could have been if we were still speaking to them, their divorce has them tied down as they continue to fight over assets.

Everyone stands when my father and I step onto the rose pedals that decorate the soft sand. I feel my stomach twisting with excitement as I let my eyes drift up to the end of the aisle where Andrew is waiting for me. His eyes are locked onto mine and his lips are spread in the biggest smile as he watches me take the last few steps towards him. I know I'll remember the way it felt for him to look at me so lovingly for the rest of my life.

As the sun sets over the ocean behind us and the sky ignites in beautiful purple and pink hues, we promise to love each other forever and to be faithful as husband and wife. Trust is not easy in the world that we live in, but trusting Andrew comes as easy to me now as breathing. I'm sure we'll have our moments where sharing our lives will be hard, but I'm confident that the love and respect that we have for each other will pull us through.